THE
CROSSROAD

THE
CROSSROAD

V Singh

PARTRIDGE
A Penguin Random House Company

Copyright © 2014 by V Singh.

ISBN: Hardcover   978-1-4828-3838-1
            Softcover   978-1-4828-3837-4
            eBook   978-1-4828-3836-7

To order additional copies of this book, contact
Partridge India
000 800 10062 62
orders.india@partridgepublishing.com

www.partridgepublishing.com/india

The story is a work of fiction. This is my first attempt and when I started writing, I never knew how it would begin and complete, and that it would take such forbearing bends. The story defies chronological order of storytelling, merging into the haze of timelessness, delving further in an untried way of first voice, with recurrent narration in different time zones.

I do not believe any of the events mentioned in the story has happened or is likely to happen. It is a story created around mysterious facts, lush interpretations, stark imaginations and stalled dreams. Resemblance to anyone real, living or dead may or may not be coincidental.

*Dedicated to my family - for their love and faith
in me helped create what I am today*

Prologue:

Lost in thought, I walked, in the dust and heat of the road, listening to my heart that was beating in despair. The road appeared long and endless. I may have covered some distance when my pace slowed down. It was as if I had walked for miles and had finally reached a turning point.

I found myself in the middle of nowhere - with no sign board or direction. A painful stagnation descended upon my soul. Unceasing flow of gleaming and intellectual people, burning with lofty ambitions were jostling for space. They were erratically moving in all directions in their quest for life - a mad pace that I probably had not been able to get on with. While these people were darting about haphazardly, I stood far behind to decide on the path that had to be taken. Amidst million drifters, I could hear echoes of my own thoughts, and from a distance I saw towering scales of insurmountable high rises. All the buildings around me were getting taller and taller trying their best to make me feel small and insignificant. With dizzying highs and depressing lows, I apprehended that it had been my descent and I had reached the nadir. Every instinct of me must have been crying, as I got fleeting glimpses from people, but it had no affect on me…

Leaving behind the reckless pursuit of a cutthroat and the so called contemporary life, it was time for me to find the real purpose of my existence. Purpose, is what I badly needed for so long. I had to start believing and thriving on hopes that I could not see earlier. I needed to desperately fight deep inside to live on.

For a long time I stood frozen. A mild wind blew past me when her words drifted on the concurrent stream of my austere thoughts. She told me once, 'often, we take life's crossroad as an end; whereas we should just consider it to be a bend and not the end.'

And here I am, beginning from the end...

THE **CROSS**ROAD

The bang broke the reverie with a rustle, as I lost control. My motorbike diverged from its path at frightening velocity and it skidded with screeching sparks in hair-raising split seconds. The roar and shriek of metal filled my ears. Screech! Bang! Thud! Like an explosion it shattered the silence of the night. Fragments of glass got shattered across and rattled on the tarmac. It caused a trail of smoke and dust to float in the air for a few seconds before settling down once again. Everything went so quiet, and so still, as if in an instant it was all over.

The oil leaked from the engine, while I was lying in a pool of blood that gushed out relentlessly from my mouth and nose. The road seemingly oozed out blood, streaming through the cracks, as if the road itself was wounded. My body temperature may have shot up, as all I could feel was only the heat. With festering wounds, peeled and burnt skin, I lay face down on one side. As the sight was fading, I could see the crack on the glass of my Casio wrist watch. It showed 22.11, and while it beeped I breathed in short buffs, the sight faded out.

After a few moments, when the sight faded in, I could feel my lungs gasping for breath and I could taste the metallic flavor of blood in my mouth. It took a while for some analytical part of my brain to realize that I had met with an accident. I tried to drag myself up but just couldn't. Locked in a surreal state and with a lot of struggle, I tried to regain my consciousness, and could somehow manage to turn around and lay on my back, on the unrelenting asphalt crossroad.

Floating in space, I could see the constellations in the sky. It was somewhat unusual. I saw the obscurity with a distant half and infertile moon, and then my eyes trailed to a new batch of stars gleaming across the horizon that was forcing me in delirium. It shattered into tiny bits like falling stars, causing sleep-inducing strain. It was a timeless descent in slow motion. I could hear her voice. She was calling my name. With sticky eyelids, my entire body shivering, I wished death upon a falling star. Meteorically the beep started fading. It was 22.18 and time was about to cease. My life was ebbing out of me... slowly I was drifting away... A rush of wind, blurred images, echoing sounds of deranged glee and it was finally the end...

Twenty Six years ago...

A new life was stirring inside a womb. Like everyone, in the form of a little embryo, I had begun my journey, and my parents believed that the most beautiful thing was about to happen.

However, during my birth there were some complications that my mom had to deal with. She found herself in hours of labor. Negotiating with sudden rain and storm, the siren howling in the dead of the night, an ambulance rushed my mom to a neonatal intensive care unit of a local government hospital that boasted of 100 beds. A major unprecedented power failure had occurred in the town. There was a complete black out... probably suggesting my arrival...!

It was dark. Even stand-by generators failed to kick-in for some reason. Doctors and nurses ran frantically to get things in place. A ward boy managed to get lanterns that came in handy in such contingent situations. While nurses piled away the bloody sheets into the corner, the hospital's magic lanterns helped the dissection and the umbilical cord was clamped and cut.

Giving birth to a child could never be easy for a mother – as it gets incredibly painful and emotionally demanding. Women swell up and become sick. It can be compared to nothing less than a miracle and it always surprised me that some women would describe the experience as 'divine'. It scared me. It scared the hell out of me when I saw it on television: a bloated woman almost split with intense menstrual cramps and exhaustive contractions, pushing and expelling the soaked baby, discharging blood and slimy substances. But then, this is how it happens, and most of us maintain that life is beautiful...

Anyways, life happened. Why? I am not sure, but it happened to me. It was an instant of glory so as to say and a miracle of a newly created life. I was born. It was a new life for my Mom as well. And like in the beginning of the world when God said, "Let there be light," and there was light, there was an emanation of light. Power resumed and the entire town was lit up once again. I was named *'Ronnak'*. It was my parent's inviolable and spur-of-the-moment choice, and this is how I was told about the night I was born and the reason for my name.

I was told I kept crying until I was wrapped in a white oblong cloth and handed over to my Mom. Her touch must have made me secure. She was filled with immense happiness. In spite of all the pain that I gave her, months of her strange imaginings and musings about what kind of a baby I would be and what kind of mother she would be, a strange awareness swamped over her life. My connection with her was evident and as a tiny clueless infant I was dependent on her for survival.

It do not remember much about my early childhood, but it always conjured up nostalgic pictures in my mind from all our family photo albums that I kept seeing during my formative years. I was extremely delighted and excited to know that a new baby was soon to come, and I kept singing in a voice of a pure hearted four year old kid near my mom's tummy. I had started developing a bond with my little sister even before she came into this world.

Then they took mom away for a couple of days. I was left at home with my grandparents. And then late one morning I was sitting on the front steps with my grandpa, waiting for mom and papa to bring our baby home. A fiat taxi chugged down the street and pulled into our driveway. I glanced up to see mom sitting in the back seat. She looked pale, but she managed to smile and wave at me. Grandpa gave me a little shove. "Go on," he said. "Go meet your little sister!" Papa opened the car door, and stepped out carrying a little bundle in his arms. He bent down to show me our sweet, delicate rosy-cheeked baby with small round eyes. I touched her thin lips with my little finger. My delight knew no bound when the baby cooed at me. She was so tiny and red... so delicate!

Raising kids needs lot of care and patience. Kids need love, and we got all of it in plenty. Growing up together was fun, though she used to get on my nerves when she kept coming in my room to disturb my stuff. I was sick of her drama. She deliberately annoyed me when I was on a call or while I was playing some game on my computer. It was utterly ridiculous. We fought like bitter enemies on several occasions over petty issues. When I would be lazing on the couch, fixated on the television, with my finger continuously jabbering the remote control buttons, she would keep pleading and yelling for her choice of channel. I wished I could point the remote control at her and just shut her up by clicking the mute button. But the mute button never worked on her. She would come and switch off the television and run away. We howled and screamed over disagreements, even at a slightest provocation. Our battles were epic. We loathed each other's presence and I felt like pulling her pony tail while she probably wanted to punch me on my nose for bullying her all the time. She was sick of my tyrannical presence. I used to keep hounding her by simply locking her wrists behind her back until they turned blue and pale. I would allow her hands to be set free only if she admitted to give up on a particular fight. Often, after the pretence of giving up, she used to come back with a vengeance, and would scratch me with her nails or pinch me as hard as she could and run away feeling rescued behind Papa. 'Grow up folks!' is what papa would say every time.

In spite of all our inane battles, our togetherness meant a lot to each other. After all we both were kids adapting with each other. Things changed and evolved as we grew, and we had grown to love each other in abundance. I knew that no matter how stupid things

I might do in my life, I would always have one fan in this world, cheering me from the sidelines. I was always protective about her and the fact remains that she always had been a great support for me. Papa was always proud of her.

It would have been the same for me, if only I had been more responsible, and not puked all over the bed after getting drunk. Since then I'd wrenched with guilt in my heart.

I had grown up but I was yet to find his acceptance. I always felt he was more concerned about what was happening in and around the world - glued to news channels and poring over newspapers for hours. He was kind of unaware of what was happening in the family, especially with me. May be he wasn't too happy with me. So many mornings, I woke up with his scolding. His strict outlook made him unapproachable, and I always found it difficult to talk to him.

I had been a repenting prodigal. I guess it was all because of my inadequate feelings and somewhat low self-esteem. Because in my heart I always knew how much he loved all of us. So many mornings, I'd seen him kissing mom to wake her up from sleep. And even though my thoughts remained unspoken, somehow I wanted to express all that I felt for him. He was always there in his own ways, to give us a secured and stable life.

There were times when I argued, disobeyed and neglected his counsel. Sharp differences in many matters divided us vertically. It was just that we both had been so different. There were times when I wanted to know his opinion - when my options were limited, and I had been uneasy about forced choices and forks in the road. When I lost my way in this deceitful world, I never consulted him. Wish we were more like friends.

I don't know if I would ever be able to tell him that I always admired him – for his simplicity, righteousness and integrity towards family and work. He'd been an epitome of honesty, an amazing person with unblemished heart and abundance of knowledge. There were so many things to learn from him.

But then, like always, I was late in learning. Though there were no unreasonable expectations that he had from me; I could not live up to them. No matter how hard I tried, I could never betray my nature, and every time I ended up being a failure. Exhausted with my foolishness, my heart had become inflamed with remorse and disgrace. Why couldn't I be the son that he wanted me to be? Why? The question nagged me profusely. I was dying, and never once in my life I made him feel proud of me... wish I could have left a written note, mentioning 'I am SORRY.'

Smeared in blood, I was rushed to the hospital with a five inch noxious gash across my forehead down to my cheek with almost every facial bone broken. My entire body was exploding in ferocious pain. Small pieces of glass had pierced my face and other body parts. Opening my eyes was a real struggle. Strange voices were all that I could hear, and those crying voices were mesmerizing. My appearance was drugged and drunken like. Then I puked some blood, and my chest pulsated violently, while I was laid flat on the bed. My stained shirt soaked in blood was ripped off and my favorite pair of jeans was pulled down to scrutinize details of injuries.

My entire body seemed paralyzed and it was menacingly real. I could not move my right hand. It had no sensation. I struggled to open my swollen eyes, but dried blood held my eyelids together. I made an effort to open but blurred vision could not bestow the picture. The light in the room was unbearable for my eyes burning with simmering temperature. All the sounds and voices were getting distorted.

It was an emergency ward and doctors were examining me, while I was lying stripped with blood oozing out of the cuts and deep wounds. I had sustained a myriad of injuries, including having inside of my mouth ripped. My skull had become dislodged. Blood pooled around my head, my ear full of blood, and it ran from my nose and mouth. The nasal bone that supports the upper portion of nose between the eyes was damaged and out of shape. Swelling and clotted blood limited the flow of air. My eyes were swollen and bulging out of the sockets with eyelids intermingled with blood that dried.

Besides broken bones, cuts and bruises, doctors were more concerned about internal injuries as they thought it might have impacted my internal organs violently. What was feared was torn blood vessels and internal bleeding. It was physically and emotionally demanding for my bereaved parents. It triggered severe anxiety in them. With my face smashed and brutally damaged, I was barely recognizable. There were so many tubes with syringes pierced in my veins. An array of lights danced overhead on the monitor's screen. Bags and bottles of fluid were hanging and running around through me, while X-rays and CT scans reports were on their way.

The cork of the champagne bottle popped with fizz bubbling all over. It was time for celebration. My face was festooned with chocolate cake. The music blasted and we all danced to the pulsating beats. It was pure youth exuberance where vague optimism ran high. Like an inspired bundle of energy, we called everyone to raise a toast! Glasses and bottles clinked with the sound of cheers!

We were ready to take some important decisions about our lives, and we were looking forward to a future that held untold promises. We were ready for the roller coaster ride called life.

Time had passed away so swiftly. Several incidences and occurrences intermingled with time blurred away and memoirs got diffused, but significant ones remained to revive quaint nostalgic memories. Those were the days where sun shined brightly on our face and we brimmed with infantile hopes.

First day in the college – I walked through the architectural grandeur of its building, and then on entering the classroom I saw my new classmates - all as strangers, some smiling nervously, some excited, others too cool for the impending introduction rituals. Noticing a few girls giggling merrily, I took a seat somewhere in the middle of the row. It was an unusual kind of a feeling where I felt socially awkward for a while. I was just a face in the sea of faces around me, and then gradually, I gained popularity.

Being genial and generous, with a great capacity for affection, I was liked by one and all. Witty humor and un-matched wisdom made me popular. I was pinned as a funny guy and I did my best to live up to my reputation. I was one of the biggest pranksters of our times. Guys found it funny even if I came up with some corny lines. Strange! I don't even know if that was worth mentioning. But the fact that I could strum the guitar, sing and entertain got me admiration as well. I would create my own compositions, and it would extremely please me to get that adulation from all my listeners.

As far as academic goes, our motto was, 'If we learn everything today, what will we learn tomorrow!' College was about being late, and then giving pathetic excuses, bunking, and sneaking out of ongoing lectures from back doors, spending time in the canteen, *cutting-chai* and all, sometimes indulging in cheap, desultory and vague discussions about meaningless plans for the day, and laughing over trite jokes, roving our eyes and rotating our heads at 360 degrees with jaws dropped while furtively and intently glancing at every nicely shaped girl with praise-worthy voluptuous curves. Appreciating beauty was not hesitated. We were prompt and natural.

Our leisurely conversations were of monumental importance, without focus, and in every direction. We despised derivatives and integration, trigonometry and calculus, assignments and theories. At times, when we had nothing to do, like devils in disguise, we would walk inside the classroom with innocent faces, and occupy the last bench. Some lectures were quite a drag to our patience, so much so, that even meritorious students felt drowsy, but our professors continued teaching economic, financial and what not theories mercilessly. And if we had some disciplinarian lecturer, we would sit with our heads bowed down, to humbly yawn and fall asleep, snore, often finding ourselves standing foolishly, clueless - like dead meat that are frozen stiff, when asked a simple question about the topic being taught. Ironically, we never felt a hint of remorse.

We indulged in a variety of extramural activities - it ranged from bike rides, volley ball, cricket, watching movies, and adventure outings, consuming copious amount of beer and rum, partying and pure enjoyment. Even though many of us faced money-crunch situations, particularly through the end of months, anytime was party time for us. And amongst all there was one bash in particular that would stay with us forever - our graduation party that coincided with my 21st birthday.

We kicked our bikes into gear and kept shuttling between different places to find a suitable venue. Being a Culinary Arts student, Mohit was refining his skills during his hands-on internship in a fine dine restaurant. That gave him a chance to network with established industry professionals. We spotted one of the plush resorts. He spoke with the banquet manager and negotiated to get our own drinks. That saved a good deal of money as no corkage was charged. We had our own bartender – Marc. He had just finished a course in bartending and was counting on successful years ahead as a high-profile bartender. We left it to him to handle the bar single handedly. So we had all kinds of liquor and juices stocked up in the boot of Mohit's car. Our planning in such matters would always be immaculate.

Sanjana took all the pain with decorating dilemmas for the banquet decked up with helium filled balloons, colorful curled ribbons and managing colorfast confetti cannons and twisters. I told her to let it be as the whole idea was kid like. She stubbornly asked me to keep quiet. I never wanted those visual effects but it was nice to see her doing all of it for sheer party delight. So all I could do was see those latex rubbers being wasted in the form of balloons.

We were all waiting for Karan. He had been my true bum chum. We grew up together and our friendship had been a legend. Karan Singh – a very intellectual, wonderful, stylish and handsome guy.

I remember our school days, when in afternoons, we use to spend our time at the terrace on the pretext of combine studies. And all we did was fly kites. Karan would manage to finish with his studies somehow, and I kept flying kites. The result was just as expected. Karan would pass out with flying colors and I would manage to get pass the examinations, yet flying colorful kites in the blue sky from the rooftops. Those colors were not meant for me but for the skies above.

I wasn't good in cricket, football, hockey, tennis, chess or anything. What I mean is that I was by no means the most popular in school. That tag belonged to Karan. He was always sure about what he wanted. Being a good sportsperson, he was captain of our school's cricket team. I too wanted to do something. When I got selected in our school's cricket team, I never missed any practice sessions. Huffed and puffed while running with the rest of the team for warm up, I could barely run for a few miles. It left me out of breath. It was physically exhausting but at least the practice sessions kept me away from studies.

I was sent as an opener in one of my debut matches and I was stumped in the first ball for stupidly playing outside the crease. In my second game I stupidly ran and got myself run out without scoring. In one of the games, I remember I was sent last and the match depended on me as we needed just one run in the last over. I got clean bowled. Because of my consistency in performance I was dropped out. It was a useless game. I simply hated cricket.

It had been almost a year to hear Karan's interesting and unusual encounters. He had this knack of regaling everyone with his amusing anecdotes. He was pursuing computer engineering, and was to reach late as he was coming all the way from Pune for the bash. There was someone special accompanying him. He had told me about this girl he had met during his second year and over a period of time both of them had started developing feelings for each other. But he wasn't too sure about it, as she was a Catholic.

All of us squealed in delight when they arrived. Karan greeted and hugged me with gusto. Standing behind him was a beautiful girl in light blue dress. She was definitely a head turner. And I could understand why Karan was so smitten by her. I noticed Nazareth when he was introducing her to everyone. She was tall, slender, and dusky with long and dark curly hair. I went up to her, and we made our introductions, shook hands, exchanged pleasantries and friendly banter. It was as though we had known each other for a long time. She was elegantly graceful with accented English. We got along well from the moment go!

The party rocked and I was the quintessential celebrity. All of us were jumping up and down in squeals of laughter. It was pure indulgence - terrific cocktails with interesting flavors ranging from champagne, tequila, rum, peach schnapps, vodka and all. You name it and we had it. Pihu ensured no one left the dance floor. She was the best DJ we could have had. Breaking the gender barrier she had created her own distinctive style. In fact she had gone overboard with the best sound and music with lasers, LED lights, mirror balls, par cans, smoke machines, truss and all that jazz. We were like livewires and the dance floor was on fire.

We felt like we had achieved it all. Life was promising and we were all set and raring to forge ahead, so we tried best to inch our ways through the maddening and cheering crowd to the bar & get a drink to lubricate our parch throats. Drinks flowed unrestrained and we drenched in it. Our spirits were panting with cries of freedom and triumph. The haze in the banquet was accentuated with our silhouettes and the machine that emanated colorful smoke added visual charm.

And then in that haze the birthday cake was bought. It was a big Swiss chocolate layered cake flavored with coffee and with dark chocolate icing. It was the most delicious looking cake, made by Sanjana. Just when the cake was about to be cut, Karan almost squeezed me with his strong embrace and then lifted me off the ground and swirled me for a few rounds. There was a confetti blast and everyone raised a toast. I blew out the candles with aplomb while I heard the most stupid song – 'Happy birthday to you!' I actually could not wait to devour it and took a big bite as if famished for days. Everyone else literally drooled with their tongues wagging out. And then something happened that was expected, I got a facial! My face was completely scrubbed with cake. Without resisting I took it flamboyantly. It was done with grace and honor - let it all come. Terence was on a photography spree. He was an aspiring photographer who knew all technicalities in the book but found it difficult to frame a perfect picture. But somehow he had managed to click some real good pictures. I guess it happened because he was drunk. He wouldn't have managed that staying sober, we'd bet.

Like true revelers we reveled till the dawn cracked. I was not sure about the amount of alcohol I must have gulped down. When you keep sipping from everyone's glass, you cannot keep a count. But still I had managed to stay up and not conk off, as I had to take care of things after the party. Though in the morning I had this somewhat muzzy feeling, it was still a matter to wonder as to where all the energy came from.

We caroused till the wee hours, and everyone left for home early in the morning. We got drowned, and with all of it drowned all the reflections of our past conduct. The resolution was in waiting. It was so tiring and the toxins in the blood spread in the entire body that it had a nauseating effect when I reached home. I entered my room to see everything in disarray, and clothes strewn all over the bed. With hormonal and biological clock imbalanced, I fell flat and crashed on the bed.

The diabolic clock kept ticking slowly and steadily. Life swung like a pendulum backward and forward between pain and little joys. And then one more year of my life lapsed, giving an eerie feeling as crucial moments were drifting away. The timepiece hadn't stopped and it kept ticking audibly in that silence, bringing me much closer to dark perilous demise.

Everyone was grief stricken and in a state of shock. The excruciating wait for my parents became endless. Their hearts died, partly with pain, partly with horror of mind, and the thoughts of what was to happen. Consumed in misery, and to put it dramatically, they saw their good looking, guitar playing kid dying in front of their helpless eyes.

Karan had also reached the hospital. He was back from London after almost a year or so. Doctors were trying their best to revive me. It was heart breaking for my parents to know in the face of hopeless prognosis that only prayers could save me. The statement had caused an alarm.

A mad rush of medical staff was wasting their time on a waste like me. The scene was pandemonium. My story had been replete with failures, and I was soon to be a cause of yet another failure for the surgeons operating on me. They should have had let me die with some leftover esteem! I was irrevocably exhausted and any more procrastination in my death would have ruptured more dignity. My life had become insignificant. The best thing for the doctors would have been to inject the vein to my heart with an empty syringe so that I could have got rid of all the agony and sobering realizations. How did I end up being such a looser? I wanted to give up, everything. I wanted to have that once in a lifetime experience – to die a brazen death.

"Get up Ronnie. Wake up!" Roshni was jostling me vigorously. She smacked me with a pillow on my face. I mumbled in deep slumber and asked her to get out of the room. Roshni shook me and said that Papa had come and everyone was ready to go for dinner. It took my brain a couple of seconds to register the time in the clock. It was 8.11 p.m. I left my yawn half way, 'Shit!' I croaked, and instantly jumped out of the bed in a flash and leapt to my feet. I groggily told Roshni to give me fifteen quick minutes for getting ready, and pleaded her out of my room. I realized that I had been sleeping since morning. Actually, I had been sleeping for eons. In a jiffy, I rushed to the bathroom and splashed water on my face. I was yet to celebrate my birthday with my family.

There was a faint and stale smell of alcohol still lingering in my mouth. I brushed my teeth quickly and cleaned my tongue. Roshni knocked on the door saying she had a t-shirt kept on the bed. Thanks! I yelled, naked in the shower scrubbing every inch of me vigorously. She left. 'Hey Roshni! I forgot my towel'!

I was out in no time. When I opened my wardrobe it was chock-a-block with an avalanche of clothes. My mom scolded me for being so messy and careless but I could hardly adhere to maintaining an order. The mess in my room always drove her crazy. But then it was such a waste of time. It would have me spend almost a day in stacking and organizing my closet, but in two days it would be in the same condition, messier than messiest. It never impaired my ability to locate what I needed amidst the pile. Though I had to riffle-raffle a bit in the process, I pulled out crisp white underwear from the stash in my wardrobe. I smelt it to make sure it was fresh. Yes it was. I sported it in a split of a second, and scrutinized myself in the mirror in my jockey, looking at my naked torso, flexing my muscles, almost convinced with myself that I had a great body. Ha!

Quickly I literally jumped into a pair of jeans lying on the floor and pulled it up to my lower waist and zipped it up. I sprayed my favorite brand of perfume. 'Hey nice t-shirt', Roshni got a new crimson red Benetton T-shirt for me. I liked the color. It looked good on me. I was out of my room in twelve minutes. While I walked towards the drawing room, Papa got up from the couch and hugged me. I touched his feet to seek his blessings and then Mom came and hugged me, kissing my forehead to bestow her blessings too.

After much deliberation, on what kind of cuisine we should try out, we froze on Mainland China. The buzz and hype surrounding the restaurant had been good, and we went there to authenticate if it was true. I was quite taken by its seductive charm until the overpriced menu was handed over. But then you don't really pay for the food but for the ambience. The walls were cluttered with oil paintings. They were quite good to look at. Roshni and I decided on the menu – and ordered for some starters to be followed by the main course considering it had fish, shrimps, chicken with a dash of rice and noodles. Roshni preferred the combination of sweet and spicy, while I was hooked on to garlic flavored sauce. I saw Papa and realized that he had something for me. He gifted me an elegant looking Casio wrist watch. I wondered how Papa knew that I was fancying on that particular model. In all probability it suggested a symbol of new time to come. Papa had always been very particular about time. In fact he disliked my habit of squandering it, and the disorientation and procrastinating attitude that was so much of an indispensable part of me. He wanted to drill this in my mind that if I did not respect time, it will also pay no reverence to me.

Time just passed by so quickly like sand drifting and slipping off from closed fist. So many times we hear that time, like tide, doesn't wait for anyone. It did not wait for me either. The world was spinning faster and faster and time was running out. When alarm rang I would hit the snooze button and go back to sleep. Sleep had been something I whole heartedly indulged in, as if it were my birth right which no one could ever take away from me. I'd never been a morning person. And I was born in a family where early rising was always considered next to Godliness. And my morning lethargies made me a sinister. But then I enjoyed being cozy in my warm covers and lolling in bed. It was better than trudging through daily routines.

Mom, Papa, Roshni and Karan had been awake for the whole night waiting anxiously. They had not eaten anything. It was very important for Mom to take care of her health. Besides being diabetic, her low blood pressure had been a cause of concern. She'd been on her daily shots of insulin to keep the glucose level under control to avoid any kind of damage to her blood vessels, nerves and tissues. She was somehow managing to go through the ordeal.

Papa kept pacing up and down. Mom was completely robbed of thoughts, expressions, and words. Faint shadows beneath her eyes and furrows between her brows and a wrinkled forehead made it visible. She was perpetually drowsy and highly distressed. She needed rest, but refused to budge, and stayed near me all the time, in spite of all the feverish turmoil within herself. Somehow, Roshni had gathered courage and was trying to take stock of the situation. She made sure that Mom took medicines on time. Karan went to the canteen located in the atrium near the reception area of the main entrance to get some sandwiches for everyone. He also got some coffee in paper cups from the dispensing machine in the corridor. Mom refused to eat anything. Roshni's insistence went in vain. Karan sat next to mom and handed over the cup and asked her to at least have coffee.

The smell of the coffee will always remain somewhat elusive. The aura of its heady, affluent aroma always brought fond memories and conjured up so many feelings. The smell of freshly brewed coffee along with the waft of warm pleasant breeze, would always remind me of her.

It was 14th of April, in a seaside café where we first met. I could feel the mild sun on my face, and could hear the sounds of the surf crashing meters away - with soft piano music resonating in the background. That's when she walked inside the café through the glass door. I noticed her over the rim of my hot and steamy coffee cup nestled in my hands.

We both were like two strangers with separate ways, who met at a virtual crossroad where our paths met. Our encounter was purely by chance – just the way it happens in movies and all - call it a strange quirk of fate; destiny, coincidence or whatever. We were perfect strangers till the haze of the hot coffee faded and we got to see each other more clearly. I guess I may have been looking at her for more than what was appropriate. Bestowing a few hasty glances, we finally got caught.

It was a chance meeting, and then one thing led to another, we exchanged our numbers, met for a couple of times more and soon realized there was something special in our meetings. In the beginning, we had our share of inhibitions but gradually it compelled us to ask ourselves why we were so deeply attracted to each other. It was something like I had experienced in my dreams umpteen times. And then upon awakening, I had never been able to retain a clear visual picture. A part of me had seen her, a part of me had not recognized her, and a part of me had waited for her. Those were enchanting emotions and the feelings that began were like an unknown mystery that kept elucidating. The strangeness and obscurity of the dream got revealed. The mystery was unveiled right near that mystic ocean and it was Nivedita. I called her Nivya.

We fell in love in that coffee shop, and we just wanted to stay together for the rest of our lives and beyond.

She was just the kind of person I wanted to be with. In fact she was more than I could have asked for. Her kohl-laden hazel eyes, her smile, her sweet lips and the smell of her skin, made me all so crazy about her. Our initial meetings were just like the song by Barbara Streisand and Bryan Adams – 'I've finally found someone'.

That song kept lingering on my mind whenever I thought about the first time we met. That's what music did to us. It always had an amplifying effect on our emotions and the loving affirmations that we had between us.

The coffee shop became our regular meeting point. Those were magical moments – piping hot and frothy coffees, elegant pastries, walnut brownies, music and above all Nivya. Life had never been so wonderful before. Everything seemed so blissful, profound and meaningful. Her presence in my life filled my heart with so much of love and gave a whole new meaning to my being. She was like an inspiration. Somehow all the uncertainties in life disappeared, and it got replaced by new found confidence and hope. It stirred up a positive emotion. And for the first time it was there – a special feeling that I had never felt before. I felt needed and desired by someone I needed and desired the most. That feeling made me feel unbelievably alive. It was my renaissance…

Once she had asked me if I believed in destiny. It was something that had never occurred to me before. I guess I had never given much thought to it earlier. But then she was correct. There had to be a purpose. And more importantly Nivya and I always felt connected from the very first moment we met. It must have been destiny that brought us together.

But then there was a turning point. Our alliance was not easy. She had told me that her parents would have in no way accepted her to be in love. They had a conservative mindset, and you know how great spirits encounter violent opposition from mediocre minds. And since she expected extreme reluctance and resistance from her parents, we found ourselves on our first cross road that opened up two ways for us. One was away from each other, taking different routes. The other was walking the unseen path together. We could have decided on the former if we hadn't had our hearts involved. We chose the latter. Being fluid about it, we found the course gracefully and with a sense of underlying oneness, we decided to walk together holding each other's hand.

It was amazing to have her hand in mine and walk. There was perfect reciprocation and moreover an undeniable connection. We found a perfect soul mate in each other. There were never enough words for me to eloquently describe the mystique of her beauty, and I kept admiring her grace and gentleness. Her inner radiance would spread whenever she smiled or said something. A novel affirmative feeling emerged whenever I looked at her. She had a deep and mysterious beauty with a sweet bulbous baby face. Her hazel green eyes were always piercingly proud and confident. The mascara on her eyes made them glow enigmatically. There was something so different about her. I could not quite put my finger on it, but her charm and effervescence had cast a spell on me. Even if I glanced away from her for a while, her sweet smile would pull me back, capturing my attention. So many times, we spent hours just looking at each other, so much so that we would forget our coffees.

Anyways, I was not too fond of coffee, till I met her. It may be blasphemy, as I always preferred a hot cup of refreshing *chai*. But then the fascination for coffee was reaching maniac proportions, and it was evident - coffee shops were sprouting everywhere, proliferating all over the places. I used to believe that life without coffee was livable. But Nivya thought otherwise. I had never seen a true coffee aficionado like her who liked to patronize at all coffee establishments. She liked spending so much of time in reading, and knowing about buying freshly roasted and ground coffees.

She educated me about some interesting facts, as how coffee was discovered by Kaldi, somewhere in the high plateaus of Ethiopia. Whatever it was, our love too must have started then, years ago, and there we were, Nivya and I, together, sharing and sipping our coffee from the same cup for the first time. Something was definitely brewing.

When she asked me the similarity between cappuccino and latte, I answered, 'Both are different from espresso!' and thought it to be witty enough. Actually, I had never cared. For me coffee was just coffee. But then she helped me differentiate between espressos and ristrettos, lattes, cappuccinos and macchiatos. Nivya always wanted me to try offbeat flavors like cinnamon, cardamom, vanilla, oranges and what not. Every time I settled for a staple cappuccino and she would still be glued in to the menu card to look for 'God knows what'. And I had to remind her that nothing in the menu had changed since she last saw it. Though I liked the way when her hair fell out from behind her ear, she didn't bother to fix it because she was too focused. I would gently take the menu from her hand, only to replace it with my hand instead. She would blush and feel so shy when I conveyed my feelings to kiss her soft lips. My love for coffee grew, vis-à-vis, my love for her. At times, we would sinfully indulge together in gorging on to walnut pastries and tantalizing scoops of vanilla ice-cream with hot melting chocolate over it.

We started considering it as our special café, where a new dream took place. A new dream of love was born, and it was born in a city where millions of dreams took birth every day. I could see enormous dream in her eyes. It gave me a sense of power to go against all odds and attain the unattainable. Nothing could stop the new energy that was stirring inside me. Undeniably, it had a magical effect on me and it instilled a new kind of flame igniting hope to an unusual echelon altogether. I got to witness love in its pure and chaste form. Such kind of love does not happen often and that was the reason every moment that we had spent together had been seared in my memory.

We spent so many evenings together, looking at the sun sinking in its crimson glory. It was our café where I had kissed her lips for the first time. I got a taste of love for the first time. Blend of colors around me were getting more glorious and vivid. Splendid skies became bluer and rich grass greener. Life was never the same before.

Talking about the time we had met, that year had been unusually draining after a hard recruiting season. My little consulting company was rapidly going downhill. I had failed in my first ever entrepreneur venture. It was a human resource consulting and recruiting agency. A few bad decisions, here and there, and because I lost some valuable clients, with no money coming for almost six months and mounting bills to pay, had to shut down the business and give up the place taken on rent, sell computers and furniture at a throw away price, leaving behind a trail of few legal ramifications. One bad move and it was all over.

I was brooding over all that was lost, and to find a way to resurrect and come out of that lean phase. My friends and well wishers suggested me to take up a job. I never wanted to do that. I always felt I was never meant for taking instructions and following. I had my reasons for it – it kind of makes one a domesticated and obedient pet. Besides, one gets lured by compensation, perks, employee benefit scheme, provident fund, medical allowances, and all those embellishments. Keep slogging all day to get heavily taxed - and then, how many actually get compensated for putting those extra hours! So much time goes in pleading for increment and promotion - being at someone's mercy was not something that I fancied. According to standard convention, job gives experience. Point taken, but I had a different take on it - that experience came through mistakes and failures. So yes, I believed in all that crap one-may-say. But yes, without deviating from the point, I guess I was in a situation where I needed to deflate ego, and accept and do as time demanded. It was an itch that I had to stop scratching. The entrepreneur bugs, which were swarming inside me, were put to sleep for some time. I was sitting in the café, going through classifieds in a newspaper for jobs. I had done my bachelor's in Business Administration. Sales profession had caught my fancy. I also considered getting into sales and pursuing MBA in Marketing. I had seen my friends breaking into the IT industry, and they were doing well. Software and technology was something that fascinated me to an extent, but not much. Banking and Finance was also an option I had, but then I could not understand, what to debit and when to credit, and even when I could manage to tally a balance sheet, it never really fascinated me. Not sure what fascinated me, I took a break. And after a sabbatical, I finally decided on event management. It was yet another paradigm shift.

I had applied in a leading event management company, and I got through. College days were slowly fading into the background. Corporate world had a new way of life, different daily routine, picking up orientation materials, new formal relationships, and formal dress code. It took me a while to acclimatize with the work environment. I had joined as a business executive - handling marketing, trade shows, product launches, corporate presentations, meetings and events. It was quite challenging, simply because the corporate clients that we were handing, had done the same events a numerous times, and on every occasion we were expected to do better and put up a more captivating show than before. We were a team of five proficient and dexterous minds making a winning combination - together taking care of marketing, operations and finance. We were expected to constantly think out of the box and come up with new ideas to capture our client's interest. Simultaneously, the company had also sponsored a six week program for newly joined executives. It was highly effective as many of the concepts were thought provoking and enhanced my skills considerably. Besides, I had Sanjay Kaul, as my mentor. He had more than nine years of event management, hospitality and marketing experience. His guidance and support came as a fine knowledge base. It made me learn a great deal in data collection and manipulation, communication and making powerful presentations.

We used to go together for meetings, and while he strode with buoyancy, I would find beads of sweat trickling down my neck with itchy collar as I was not used to wearing ties adorning the cologne sprayed pinstriped creaseless shirts. While I would try to count pennies in my barely noticeable jaded trouser pocket, the martinis and exotic cuisines at so called quintessential 'power lunches', were paid by him with numerous credit cards he had in his wallet, saving generous tax deductions for the company, and then he used to get those bills reimbursed from the accounts department at the end of the month. Those expenses on traveling and entertainment were all sort of economic indicator that things were going well, and all of those frills were much more expensive than the meager salary that I earned after all the slogging. At times, I deeply felt that those tables filled with rich food and wine, were flattering in abundance. But then how would that have mattered when business was thriving.

Most of the times we closed deals, and when we came out of meetings, I would immediately loosen my tie, feeling a sense of freedom with victory gleaming in my eyes. Sanjay had simply been a genius and I would observe him closely while giving presentations in an absolute smooth and glitzy style, and the versatility that he displayed in handling different breeds of clients. It was a treat to watch his negotiation skills, without plunging into a deluge of words and wasting much time, he told me one of the golden rules of being an expert negotiator - that is to be able to walk out from the negotiating table. I still remember one of the meetings where a sucker like me would have given into a client's demand, but he said, 'I'm sorry if you misunderstood me. This is not a negotiation as we're here to simply explain our situation, so that you can make a decision in your best interest …' Impressive! Huh! He would actually leave no room for me to say much in a meeting, but I felt a sense of pride when I came up with a suggestion or two, to score those brownie points.

I was good at designing and implementing shows and events, coming with ideas to impress clients and media, sometimes introducing gimmicks, spoofs and overbearing themes taking client's requirements into considerations. Some of them were so absurd that they would get rejected outright. But ideas never stopped as the young lot was expected to keep coming up with igneous ways, round the clock.

The rawness that was clearly visible at the commencement of our training program changed. It did not transform me as a person, but more importantly it clearly defined where I stood and what I had to achieve. Our company was doing extremely good as it could boost some varied interesting clientele, nevertheless with a great potential for volume growth.

In the mean time, Nivya and I started getting closer by every passing day. We were in complete awe with each other. We shared everything. Folks at home where happy and had faith in me for the leaps that I was trying to take in my career. I had joined an MBA course that I was pursuing simultaneously with my job. Those were times when I worked awfully hard – work, reports, studies, assignments… it all kicked into full-gear!

The days kept creeping and after every hard working day I would see Nivya and my weary thoughts would take wings and fly away. She loved waiting for me at 'our' coffee shop. Yes, it was kind of amazing as we had started calling it as 'ours'. She would often spend time there in the evening listening to her choice of new age music, and reading books. It was always nice to see her and I was absolutely smitten by her sheer presence. Her bright and curious eyes with an inimitable glow on her face would tell me that there was nothing to worry about. I would rest my head on her lap and she caressed my face and her hands never stopped to gently stroke my hair. She said she loved it when I fell on her lap like a baby. She would gently massage my brows and temple, and it had a soothing effect giving incredible comfort. Her touch was magical.

There were no litanies of complaints that I wasn't able to give much time to her. Two things that she liked about me in specific were my eyes and my hands – she felt they were clear evidences of how much I loved her. The way I looked at her and the way I touched her was something she always craved for. Her words invoked confidence in me.

She maintained a diary, and shared with me interesting quotes, anecdotes and stories that she read or came across. One in particular that she told me once was, "It's better to be a failure in something you enjoy rather than being successful in doing something you hate." That statement actually made lot of sense. Her presence and love always guided me through the toughest part, and her faith in me taught me to face my fears. With divine feelings, we were harboring true definition of love in our hearts. I was so alive and passionate about my work, life and about our dream to settle together.

Also, what made me wonder was how I got so comfortable with her in no time. During college days, I used to be nervous, and lacked confidence big time while talking to girls. I used to be shy. During my childhood I would hide behind the curtain if there were guests at our place. I would fear they would ask me something. All I needed was to run to my mom and be in her embrace, but I would keep standing timidly behind the curtain hiding myself waiting for the guests to leave, so that when they would leave, I could reach her. Anyways, I know it was silly, and then I had grown out of my shyness, even though I was still a succinct and simple guy.

I had seen a lot of lousy so called lovers during my college days. They would get on with their phony relationship. Most of them were victims of fragile egos and all that I had witnessed was not love, but ridiculous manifestations of 'love', and that was something that had kept me away from any kind of commitment and relationship.

The first person to know about Nivedita was Karan. He was back after completing his engineering from Pune. He had got a placement in a prominent software company. We met on a Saturday night and went to '*Chumu da dhaba*'. This had been one of our favorite hangouts - an unpretentious place, always bustling with people even past midnight, serving gamut of authentic and lip-smacking Punjabi cuisine. The basic décor with green and yellow lights on the canopy outside gave it a somewhat rural feel, with wooden top tables and *char payees* laid out and pillows strewn around. It permitted getting your own drink. The food was surprisingly cheap compared to the rich taste it had to offer. However, we always used to buy drinks from the same place as it did not really make much of a difference. We occupied a comparatively quieter place in the corner. Karan very sweetly called the slowcoach waiter, "*oye chottu! Ithe aa*". The little boy was all smiles and strolled over to the table at once. Karan asked for half a bottle of vodka and one full tandoori chicken for starter.

We were just chatting in general and our table was filled with drinks, ice box, peanuts and a palate full of freshly cut radish, carrot and cucumber. While I sprinkled salt, black pepper, squeezing lemon juice abundantly all over the fresh salad, Karan made two large pegs of vodka with soda and dipped sliced green chilies in each glass. Cheers! We finished our first peg in a few quick sips. Hot tandoori was spicy and deliciously marinated, oozing melted butter. As Alfred Hitchcock had mentioned somewhere that conversation is the enemy of good wine and food - we stopped caring to talk and started relishing food. We were literally pouncing on the leg and breast pieces with both hands, and tearing them apart and chomping at the flesh, hankering for more. We enjoyed every bit of its tenderness, and almost moaned in delight.

And then after a while when our empty stomachs got slightly pleased, we started discussing matters of heart. A peg or two of vodka just does the trick to let surface the hidden emotions. It opened our hearts and our mouths.

Karan had issues at home with his father after discussing about Nazareth. A Sikh guy marrying a Catholic girl was not easy and Karan had anticipated smoldering resentment. Even Nazareth was facing severe flak from her folks at her place. For a person like Karan, religion held no real purpose. According to him time had changed and religion was nothing but a worn out chapter in the history of human ego. Every religion has its own belief systems. Some religions believe in the doctrine of original sin that every child is born tainted with the sin of Adam's disobedience to God; and some believe that every child is born into a state of purity, obedient to Him. Some believe in reincarnation and karmic life and all that. Neither Karan, nor I understood such institutions formulated centuries ago. We strongly felt that all the racial fanatics have always been nothing but a dreadful disease to mankind and civilization. And then it gets difficult to believe that there is only one God governing the entire world, because had that been so, we all would have been connected. We create our own Gods, our own beliefs.

Anyways, I was happy that Karan was determined to get married to Nazareth. I always liked her. For Karan, it was a matter of commitment and he was committed to Nazareth and most importantly himself. They both had spent considerable time together and were intensely in love with each other. I was proud to see my friend's brave and big heart. And as always I trusted him for his decision, though he himself had a little doubt. That dilemma was bound to be there as his parents were not at all happy to know about his choice. They thought it would bring shame and disgrace to their family and community. Besides, Karan's father never wanted him to pursue engineering as he felt his son could always join the family retail business of automobile spare parts. And above all Karan's father wanted him to marry some Dilpreet Kaur. The problem was not with Dilpreet, but Karan had never imagined himself sitting in a shop selling spares. Karan's elder brother was doing well in helping his father in their business. Karan vehemently denied his father's suggestion. He always believed in his potential and wanted to explore different avenues. He would always get animated and zealous talking about things that he would love to do. I wondered what had happened to my passion. In fact it even made me doubt if I actually had one. A guitar lying in the corner of my room flashed and faded in my mind. I thought about my Papa at that time, and felt that Karan and I were replaced as sons. My Papa would have loved him as a son. And the lazy me, would have been more than happy to be sitting at the shop minding and managing my own business and I would still find time to go to the terrace and fly kites. I thought I would not even mind to sport those lustrous beard and moustaches which Sikhs do. And then I'd seen Sikh guys getting married to beautiful Punjabi damsels. Wasn't it all worth it?

The succulent tandoori was reduced to mere shreds of bones, and we licked the remnants from our fingers. When it came to eating, we actually did not mind our table manners. Eating tandoori chicken with knife and fork can be utterly unsophisticated. And then, what's more important is to enjoy food thoroughly, and we had just finished with starters and the main course was yet to be served. We had ordered some kebabs and chicken curry with khasta roti – an ajwain flavored wheat bread baked in tandoor.

Dabbing our hands and mouth with napkins, we got back to our conversation. I told Karan that he had to be sure of Nazareth, as a lot depended on her. Karan told me that, although she'd been tender looking with an immaculate sweet voice, was very strong willed and practical as a person. She had taken her time, considering all the repercussions, and had finally made a firm decision.

She had told Karan that she would leave everything to be with him - as and when the time would demand. It was not just about a burning desire between them, but love in its true manifestation. Rare thing and I could relate to him. It was nice to know how they loved each other so much, just the way Nivya and I loved each other.

Vodka was doing its magic. The conversation veered towards Nivedita, and he was pleasantly surprised and happy. He was eager to know more. I told him that we had not proposed each other or anything of that sort but then the feelings were obvious. I guess he understood how it is when it begins. We had just started, and the feeling had been wonderful.

However, I confided in Karan that his story had more complexities and hurdles than mine. We decided that we will follow our hearts. I told Karan that Nazareth was beautiful. Besides, she was thoughtful and polite. Together they looked nice as a couple. I told him, I was imagining the hybrid generation to follow, and while saying so, I could see my buddy blushing. We cheered and hugged each other. 'One more peg!' We cheered. By then the food was also served. I guess the alcohol level in the blood was rising.

Circling the rim of his glass with his finger contemplatively, Karan said that it wasn't all that fascinating or romantic as it seemed or sounded to be. Ironically, Karan's mom was not at all pleased with his choice. He respected his parents and never intended to hurt their feelings. He wanted their consent and happiness as well. He was in a big dilemma. His parents were not ready to accept Nazareth. He could not leave her either. He sat quietly for a while with a serious expression – something that I'd never seen on his face earlier. He said he loved her and could not imagine spending even a single day without talking to her. Clearing the lump in his throat, he wiped a tear with the back of his hand. I too for a moment felt how it would be to lose Nivya. It was an absolutely unpleasant thought. Though in my case there would have been no objection from my parents as Nivya and I belonged to the same caste. But we cared a damn for religion. Life's disappointments could get so hard to take when you don't use swear words. Although I knew many, I refrained. Anyways, taking our conversation further, we discussed our lives, decisions and aspirations while we finished eating.

We burped in unison after being down with a few pegs. I snapped out of my cogitation and excused myself to go to toilet. The very fact that I could walk straight till the toilet, unzip, hold and pee in the pot with precision, without spilling, meant I could gulp another peg. When I came back I saw Karan spread on the charpaee gazing at the nameless stars gleaming above. He looked like a stellar thinker while he gazed for what seemed like an eternity at one star in particular. Without disturbing, I tiptoed my way consciously and sat quietly before pouring our last pegs with precise measure. I too spread myself on the charpaee. Noticing Karan gazing above, I too looked above. The moon seemed brighter than ever before. It was amazing. I made a pair of binoculars with both hands and scanned the sky. Like true astronomers we were kind of interpreting the constellations differently. A new batch of stars was gleaming across the horizon. I searched for Nivya in the sky. I had to squeeze my eyes in an effort to see her more clearly and there she was shinning bright. Onlookers must have felt we were crack from the mind, but who cared for those lesser mortals. We were overflowing with superfluous hopes in our hearts. And all we did for good sometime in silence was gaze at the sky.

The next day when I met Nivya in the café, I told her about Nazareth and Karan. She was besieged to hear their story. We held each other's hand and prayed for their togetherness. We prayed to God to guide them, and while we did that we prayed for our togetherness too, wordlessly. The beauty of that moment was enhanced by the gentle evening breeze and the sound of the distant ocean. We were holding each other's hands and praying. It was done with an element of silence and that had so much of substance.

Nivya was pursuing interior decoration and was in her final year. She had a very good academic record and gave high importance to education. She excelled in her assignments and exams, emerging as a topper for the past two years; and as always wanted to give her best for the final. I got involved and immersed in my hectic work, though I did not accomplish substantially but I was spending a lot of time in office, interacting with colleagues, coordinating and following up with the clients, meeting visitors, dashing emails, and of course amongst all this there were series of mistakes of petite and paramount proportions, promising undeliverable, taking exit points just to get out of a no-win situation and eventually getting laid in the trap, trying hard each time to adapt to business demands and latest technology, followed by firings over things I badly screwed up. All the management concepts went for a toss when implementing them in reality. Without getting much into its details, there was one event in particular that I was heading and it shot 300% over budget. Result – it never saw light of the day. Company suffered time and money. And it goes without saying; my 'case' was taken royally. Needless to say what 'case' meant in such context. Everyone screws up at some point or the other. To err is human, so I screwed up more. I was being too humane. May be I was learning more. Even when I did a wonderful job, appreciation would always shy away from me. So screwing up continued for some time till I attained perfection in my job and acquired an arsenal of skills, and then when I reached that stage, there was no time to rest on my laurels, but to move on.

Almost seven months had passed; and we constantly plotted and planned to meet on every possible occasion. I had not expressed my feelings for her profusely, but we knew we were in love with each other since the time we first met. Nivya wanted to hear it from me for a long time. Since I felt it to be very special, I was waiting for the right time. It was kind of funny as I knew it was crucial to say the right thing at the right time. So crucial, in fact, that I even hesitated, for the fear of saying the wrong thing at the wrong time. But then Nivya had realized how much I loved her. There was always this certain magnetism and enchantment between us.

But yes the fact of the matter was also that during those days I was struggling with my job and studies, and she too, had to finish her final year and internship. I had started saving money and stopped splurging it on unnecessary things as I wanted to buy a new house of our own before marriage. Anyways, I was no exception as there were so many people living in the city struggling much more and going through the pits. My situation had been far better.

I started exploring the real estate market and the sky-rocketing prices of properties were quite a dampener. Concrete tall buildings burgeoning everywhere would try to make me feel smaller. Buying outright was just impossible and the loan would have eaten up all my salary in equated monthly installment. But I did not let those tall buildings to grow beyond my reach. Not being too rich did not swallow my pride and I never allowed it to wilt my pursuit and I kept thinking about the ways to get there! I kept seeing innumerous apartments – some built, some semi built and some under construction. I knew it was just a matter of time that I would be able to buy a house of my own. It was the beginning of my career. We had time.

But then time was actually running out. There was a fear that if I remained in the same state, it could lead to severe disability. My left part of the body was not responding. While the team was performing a thorough examination, Dr. Nirav Sahai, the neurologist was waiting for the Commuted Tomography – (CT) scan report in particular as he suspected some clot in the brain arteries. He cleared his throat and explained to my parents that my brain needed oxygen to survive - the blood carries oxygen and other important nutrients to the brain and if a part of brain does not receive oxygen for a certain amount of time, the tissue in that part of the brain can get damaged and can die. Hence, to prevent blood platelets from clumping together to form a clot, blood-thinning aspirin was administered. The team was trying hard to prevent fever and keep the sugar levels in the blood at normal. Papa wanted to know the consequence. Doctors found it difficult to tell that it could affect vision, speech, behavior, ability to think or paralysis for life. They said it could even cause comma or death. The statement left my Papa cold and insipid.

Papa needed a break. It had been a long time since my parents had gone anywhere. Mom and Papa were going out of town for a couple of days to attend some wedding in Gurgaon. Roshni and I decided to stay back home like good kids. Roshni was in college, attending lectures. I had taken half day as an off from work. We got stuck in the traffic on our way to Mumbai Central station. Papa was already angry with me, as I had reached late to fetch them from home. But then I had to meet Nivya. It was so important. I had not seen her for two days, and I was missing her like crazy. I felt an urge to tell Papa about her, as it was sure to cool him off. My parents would have felt happy to know about it. But it would have been too early, so I kept mum. And all of a sudden, the car's air condition that was running just fine till then started malfunctioning. Cooling was not sufficient. It just added fuel to fire. Papa got hyper. I tried to play with the fan, switched on and off the air condition button several times, but nothing happened. And that triggered a long lecture about my callous attitude of not valuing and being unconcerned about things that I get easily. He always felt that I did not maintain the car the way I was supposed to. The only way to sabotage the situation was to just listen to everything passively for some time and appear suitably contrite. Mom did well in diverting Papa's attention by talking about our relatives who were supposed to reach for the wedding. It came as a relief. Making way through the traffic with exemplary lane cuttings and violating most traffic rules, more importantly without Papa noticing it, I managed to pull up the car at the ubiquitous parking lot, just outside the railway station, somehow in time! While unloading luggage from the car, Mom gave me clear instructions to pay the milkman, and also pay for electricity and phone bills on time. Papa informed me about the mounting phone bills that had to be kept under check. I nodded in agreement. He then inquired about where the calls were being made. I told him I was not too sure about it as I hardly made calls from our landline number. He always looked at me with so much of suspicion. I locked the boot and doors. Wheeling the suitcases along, we walked towards the station.

The platform as usual, was chaotic as the train had already arrived. I got myself a platform ticket. Being late and carrying enormous luggage is something my family always found difficult to desist. I carried two of the heavy suitcases, and we made our way through the maddening passengers trotting up and down. And amongst the melee of vendors selling mineral water, newspaper and periodicals, we reached the compartment. Earsplitting announcements barely decipherable blared from the loudspeakers and the voice crackled with static interference. I wondered what that lady, with her faster-than-train rate of speech and shrill voice, was so excited about! Anyways, while Papa checked the reservation chart on display, I scrambled into the air conditioned 2-tier sleeper class, paved the narrow passage and hogged the berths that belonged to us, stowing the suitcases beneath, and chaining them together. Mom took the seat besides the window and Papa had come in by then. They made themselves comfortable. A quick glance at fellow passengers and they seemed like a couple of the same age group, and Papa had already made an overture towards them. The two berths on the other side of the aisle were not yet occupied.

Wishing them a nice and safe journey, I gave Mom and Papa appropriate last minute instructions on how to use mobile phone to stay in contact. Mom and Papa hugged me. They were looking genuinely concerned. I told them that Roshni and I would manage. It was just a matter of few days. The train lurched forward, and I got down in a hurry to see the train clanking out of the station slowly till it was out of sight. And then all I had to do was drive back all the way home, in traffic for more than an hour. I got in the car, igniting the engine. And when I tried pressing the button for air conditioning, the cool air started billowing from the vent. It worked. Damn it!

Nivya called up while I was driving back home, and asked if we could meet. I felt an onrush of strange excitement. Nivya's parents had gone to some club for some function, and were expected to come back home by nine or something in the evening. So we had some good time to spend together. Our lives had been busy. It was never easy for us to manage adequate time together for some reason or the other. I drove till Worli where she lived, to pick her up. And there she was elegant as ever, wearing a red silk kurti and white leggings. I always liked the way she effortlessly carried herself. It had so much of grace and refinement. Her eyes, ever-so-mysterious, were so intense. I was awestruck. The predominant thought in my mind after looking at her was 'Wow!'

It was our first drive together. Obviously one of my best drives and I whole heartedly enjoyed bumper to bumper traffic. Whenever with Nivya, I drove with care. And then, there was traffic and perfect chaos and we loved every bit of it. We were in no hurry at all. Strange but true – I used to hate being in traffic but then it was just so romantic - Nivya besides me in the passenger seat, while we were listening to some quixotic songs that captured our spirit and fervor that was budding inside us.

Looking forward to a good evening, our conversation remained chirpy, bright and lively. When we turned left from Walkeshwar towards Marine Drive, traffic vanished and the drive got better with six lane concrete road. We personally felt that the long graceful boulevard along the coast in South Mumbai was the best part of the city, known as Queen's necklace, simply because, if one looked at it at night from an elevated angel, the glittering street lights along the drive resembled a string of pearls. We could see the sedative sun setting, with its light glinting off the sea. Nivya just loved it, and it was delightful to see her enjoying all of it.

I could imagine all of it in slow motion. We had reached the far end of Nariman point, and got down from the car, and saw a flurry of pigeons with the setting off sound of their wings flapping, rising from the sidewalk. The wind was soft and warm, whispering its way across. The place was swarming with pedestrians and cars and motorcycles, and pavement was filled with vendors displaying trinkets, colorful balloons, candy floss, chickpeas, groundnuts, popcorns, cold drinks and all. Nivya saw corn cobs being roasted and sizzling on the charcoal at a distance. I never knew she was so fond of it and its palate-tickling aroma was simply hard for her to resist the temptation. We went to one of the road side hawkers, to grab a bite of blissfully burnt yet juicy '*bhutta*'. Looking at the way she enjoyed eating it made me enjoy it too, though I found it spicy. It was all buttered, and slathered with salt, red hot chilies and lemon. Nivya was never bothered about calorie-count, especially when it came to sacrificing zesty flavor. There was actually no need, as she was petite enough and I would have never minded her putting on some flab. Wafer-thin anorexic girls had never been my type. I was just looking at Nivya devouring succulent *bhutta* and I wished I was a *bhutta* then.

I was wondering how she could relish something so spicy. I shouldn't have tried to test my endurance or simply be macho. I realized that a man's pride could get him in a lot of trouble at times. Although, I had relished eating spicy yet delicious bhutta, after a while, I relinquished as it was driving me crazy and I was going ballistic with watery eyes and entire face quenched up, getting redder by the second! I was fanning my mouth with fast waving hands. It was kind of funny. Nivya was trying hard to suppress her laughter and offered her handkerchief and I literally blew my nose in it. I still have that hanky. She never took it back. She was literally in splits to see all of my expressions. She got a bottle of water. I took some quick sips and felt better. It had caused so much of upheavals in her belly. The laughter must have hit a 6.0 on the Richter scale. It took a while and I could regain my composure completely, only after sipping some coconut water. That gave much relief.

We strode hand-in-hand along the promenade, walking the walk, talking the talk, and giggling the giggle, smitten by the evening replete with magical moments. Letting go of her hand, I encircled her waist with my arm. She found it ticklish. And then her laugh faded away to an almost imperceptible curl of the lip. And as we walked we were oblivious to people around.

Later, we sat on the parapet besides each other with our feet dangling, looking at the beautiful large cement tetra pods separating water and land, arched along the shoreline overlooking the vast ocean. The city was silent except for the lapping of the waves and the sound of occasional vehicles zooming past by. We were watching the beautiful sun settling down. It was stupendous to behold. There was not a single disgruntled wave as far as the eye could see. A gentle sea wind ruffled her open hair. It picked up a few wayward strands of her dark brown hair and scattered them across her face. I wrapped my arms around her shoulders and drew her closer. She confessed that she felt butterflies in her stomach when I touched her. Long tendrils of her mesmerizing hair caressed my face, and I could smell the light dash of perfume she was wearing. For once, I turned to bury my face in her cascading hair and immersed myself in the giddy pleasure of her feminine smell. We were truly in a fog of emotions, contemplating how we were connected to each other.

She said that she had always longed for a special someone in her life, as being an only child was a very lonely existence. She expressed her likeness for me, as never for a moment had she felt awkward to be with me. It was all as if we knew each other for so many years. She could be herself. There was some silence between us, but it wasn't awkward at all. We were savoring that moment. Gently rubbing her arm, I told her she was not alone anymore and that I would always be there for her. She asked me for a promise to be her friend always. I told her that I would always be there, more than a friend. Her eyes were moist. She gently placed her head over my shoulder, cuddled under my chin, holding my hand. Years of crests and waves when we were unaware of each other's existence had gone by. I told her that I always wanted someone like her. At my own slow pace I told her in a tender most manner that how I had envisaged spending the rest of my life with her. I had proposed her… in a way that even I had not imagined. It was a well considered decision yet had an element of spontaneity in it. We knew we were meant for each other since the time we'd first met. She was extremely happy.

We were captivated by the mystique and splendor of the ocean, and gazed earnestly at the gentle salty froth eternally caressing the rocks on the shore. We sat there watching the sun immerse in sea, and in the haze of twilight, neon signs and street lights went up to illuminate the city. I breathed a silent prayer. We were enjoying the serenity of air filled with promise and comfort of cool breeze when a funny tone pierced the air. It was her mobile phone. Why? She pulled herself, gently off my arms and fumbled for her mobile in her bag. Her mom had called up and Nivya had to lie that she was with her friend, and would soon be home. Her parents were to reach home in sometime, which meant that it was time for us to leave. They say all good things come to an end but here it was a beautiful evening; the day was ending much better than the way it had begun.

Later in the evening, when I reached home I was quite happy. Roshni had been waiting for me. She was talking to someone over the phone, when she disconnected on seeing me. The entire day had been hectic since morning and it urged me to take a quick shower. In no time I was fresh and in casuals. After a long time, we got a chance to spend some time together. Surprisingly, without any arguments we watched some programs on the television together. Fortunately, our likings matched when it came to our favorite television shows and movies.

Since I had been battling a craving for Chinese food for over a week, I asked her if she could prepare it at home. Roshni made the most amazing chicken chilies and fried rice. This was something she has inherited from my granny who used to diligently cook variety of delicious food. Mom too, cooked exceptionally well. Anyways, I knew it would come for a price, so I offered Roshni help in the kitchen while cooking and with doing up dishes as well. She agreed. She checked and found frozen chicken in the refrigerator. That saved my trip to the market. In whatever capacity I could, I helped her in the kitchen. Actually, I was an absolute mess when it came to kitchen chores. Ouch! I got my head hit on one of the filing cabinet doors, when trying to get a pan out. Luckily no bump erupted and it turned out to be a not so serious hit. Roshni started chopping cabbage and capsicum and asked me to get the noodles and rice for boiling. I did as I was told and then tried my awkward hands in chopping vegetables. Ah! I can't do it! Roshni warned me to hold the knife properly or else … and I managed to slice open my index finger instead of the onion. Blood started oozing out. Roshni got really dramatic as she was too scared to see blood. She got so tensed – wide eyes full of concern and mouth open as if she had received the biggest shock of her life. She held my hands in cold running water from the tap. I told her to relax as it was just a minor cut. Without delay, she got a band aid from somewhere in mom's room, and got it stuck nicely on the cut. I told her how careful I was to not bleed over what was already cut. Ready for cooking, again!

Roshni took the knife from my hand and demonstrated her skills, telling me how to cut a round food into half and then placing the food flat-side down so that it cannot shift or roll. To hold fingers out of the way of the food by either holding the food with your fingertips behind the knuckles or with knuckles themselves. How easy! I said.

And then all I was doing was arranging the right utensils and appliances in place for cooking. God! I never knew where half the things were kept, and all of it so painstakingly hidden in so many cabinets and cantilevered shelves. How do they manage? By the time I got all the ingredients out of the refrigerator, the roasting pan was already sizzling with fresh cabbage and some spices. I was already so hungry. Roshni managed to do it all so quick, and I did well in wiping up spills, warbling and swooping precariously the cooking platform. Roshni announced that meal was ready.

And there we were, ready to binge. It reminded me that I never asked Nivya about cooking. As if, it would have made any difference. I told Roshni about Nivya. Roshni was very excited. She said that she had a hint about it. She was happy to hear that her brother was finally seeing someone. Roshni inquired if we were really serious about each other. 'Obviously' I said. But then I realized that I actually had no clue. I had not known much about her. But then how much can one know someone to be in love with. I had not met her family. I had no clue how her parents would be and things about her home. It was important to know all of that, but then not really important. I told Roshni that it was always a beautiful feeling to be with her and I found her company very amusing. She was a perfect blend of traditional and modern values. I told Roshni that she would get along and acquaint herself well with our family. Roshni was happy for me, and wanted to meet her soon.

We spoke for a long time, till around 2.00 am. Roshni was listening to me most of the time and I felt like she wanted to tell me something. I asked her what it was. She took her time and after a while revealed that she too was in love with someone. At first I couldn't believe what I was hearing. I was flabbergasted. It wasn't pleasing to the ears at all and I found it difficult to believe. How could she? She was such a kid, may be not, but then how could she do something like that! I was not even ready to listen to her and warned her to stay away from such things. Papa would never approve it and there was no way that she could seek my consent on this. There was silence. Roshni may have expected some kind of resentment from me but at least not the way I reacted. I did not even bother to ask about the guy. I felt she was too young to be in love with someone. I knew my thoughts were dense. I scolded her and told her that I won't support her for her endeavor. My remarks had wounded her precious pride and her sentiments. I told her it was too late and that she should sleep. She went to her room and threw herself across the bed and wept in despair. I sat on the couch for a while and kept thinking about it. I realized that I should not have behaved the way I did. I failed to listen to her. A stifling wave of remorse swept over me and I timidly walked in her room and found that she had fallen asleep with her head stuck under the pillow. I guess she was crying. I should have gone to her and talked. More than talking I should have listened to her. That would have made her feel better. But I did not.

She hugged me and asked me to keep her wrapped in her arms for some time. I was nonplussed for a moment. I held Nivya close to me and she held on to me firmly and buried her face into my neck. I asked her what was worrying her. She said her family is shifting base to Delhi. She had hinted something like this to happen before. But had also mentioned that she might stay back to complete her studies. Her parents wanted Nivya to move along with them. Nivya's father had decided to shift to Delhi as all their relatives were based there and he was more acquainted to that city as he had lived his early years there. The family has decided to move. Nivya told me that she will be with me every moment and that we will always be together. We were determined; however, the separation was our first trial.

Nivya left for Delhi. It took a while to digest the fact that she had moved far away. Her memory became companion to my thoughts. Days seemed like years and time went by slowly. We kept in touch daily. I would call her late at nights when her parents were asleep. I slept and woke with thoughts of her. We had a sense of separation in our hearts. Surreptitious calls and emails were the only means to make ourselves feel close to each other. Sometimes, I skipped calling her when I was busy at work. And then when I had the time to call her, she was not in a situation to take my calls. She had to keep our relationship discreet, as her parents would have felt betrayed. I too, felt that a right time would come, and we were waiting for that. Both of us wanted to settle down with our career.

She became every reason and every hope that I'd ever had. We had a sense of direction... a purpose, something just so essential.

Every moment of mine was painted in love. The more I thought about her, the more she dominated my thoughts. I would go to our café that kept exuding her essence. I would spend time alone, thinking about her, looking at the empty chair next to the table and imagine her sitting like an unassuming angel. It reminded me of her long hair and how I would lean on it and smell it. Her aroma permeated the surrounding air, while the coffee machine whirred and whooshed in the background. I found myself to be in a constant state of bliss. And then I had this tall glass of cold coffee to relish – it was drenched with chocolate sauce and topped up with whipped cream and coffee beans. I missed Nivya.

There wouldn't be a day or phase when I did not think of her. Everything kept reminding me of her - when I passed by a coffee shop, sipped coffee, saw chocolates and ice creams, when it rained, and then when I sulked in silence after a downpour that drenched the thick foliage. I would see her reflection in the rivulet of water running silently along the way. I could feel her in music that became an integral part of me. I kept listening to it wherever I went. Thinking about her I would walk along the seafront during high tide; the waves would climb the sea wall and spray salty frothy water over me. I could see us in every couple that I met. I pictured her when I would see flowers, when I would see a beautiful painting, when I would hear a prayer being recited, when I would see kids playing, when I would see gentle waves caressing rocks on the shore, when I walked down a lonely street, when I walked past a movie hall, when I smelt hot popcorns, when I crossed a mall - looking at mannequins standing tall in window displays adorning designer wears, and then when I simply looked at the empty sky above, this and that, everything reminded me of her. I was absorbing the sights, the sounds and the smells around me.

I remember it was the first time that I visited an art gallery and saw creative designs perfectly captured in brilliant colors. It left me out of breath to see beautiful paintings and enchanting sculptures of primordial elegance that were produced with so much precision and gorgeousness. It was awe inspiring. The exhibition showcased all that the artiste believed in. When I walked closer to an oil painting adorning the wall I realized how it was created - by individual and careful stroke and caress of the brush along with blend of colors. And then I heard a visitor inquiring. The gallery space had been the most sought after for upcoming artistes – and they had to wait for a good couple of years to get that space to showcase their talent. It needed time and patience. I made a mental note to keep visiting such art galleries frequently. I left from there inspired.

It enthralled me when I saw work of gothic architect and enchanting contemporary structures while crossing different streets. I kept walking. It was molding my character and belief.

It filled me with a desire to produce something beautiful and creative. An art well exhibited always tells a magnificent story. The driving ardor inside was manifesting intrinsic creative desires in me. I wanted to do something really substantial in life, and carve a niche for myself, along with Nivya. I thought about the guitar in my room. It had been abandoned for years. I wished I hadn't stopped playing. I shouldn't have given up. Music had been my passion but somewhere I had lost it...

But then life was on a move and I was fostering new imaginations. In spite of Nivya being far away, her presence in my life was inspiring. The distance between us was not a deterrent. On the contrary it bought us closer to each other. We would talk for hours together. We could talk all night till wee hours when the birds started chirping reminding us that we needed to catch a wink as well. Though talking over the phone made emotional closeness possible, but we craved for each other's touch and comfort. We would send each other text messages to communicate our tendermost feelings. At times, we would just give each other missed calls, to convey that we were missing each other.

We nurtured a dream. She liked talking about how our wedding night would be... We dreamt about the velvet night to be the most beautiful, with stars spangled, illuminated with soft gibbous moon. I experienced love in its truest form - so pure and chaste. We desired to make love all night kissing each other with affection all over. We opened our hearts to each other and expressed our feelings unrestrained. We understood each other perfectly. Those were amazing intimacies of our imaginations, emotions and thoughts, body and spirit, mind and soul. Nivya had even thought of the names that we would have for our kids. One day she asked me, 'What would it be like when we would be in the family way? Would you still love me, when I would put on weight and have a swollen tummy?' I smiled and told her that with our baby in her tummy, my love would grow for her even more. Kissing her tummy gently, I would lay there next to her propped up on one elbow and watch her sleep. She felt the urge to hug me closely. Those were some incredible moments that I would never be able to forget all my life. I treasured all her sweet whispers, her fragrance in my breath and the way she took my name in hushed way, touched my raw nerve every time. I could sense her breath in the silence of our nights. Those nights kept drifting and days would climb the mountain of time. Bright days would become somber nights and then there were also times which were a bit rough for us, but we sailed through. She would encourage me when I was crestfallen and her words were soothing comfort. We helped each other in trouncing all odds that came our way. Days just passed by and life went on. I would close my eyes, listening to the city stirring into life.

We would talk about almost anything and everything. There were times when we had squeals of laughter. I simply loved the way she laughed at all my crazy ideas. Her laughter never stopped. She would stop momentarily, and then laugh again brimming in love. Nothing else could give me such immense happiness. It made me feel so nice to know that I could make her laugh and it nourished my feeling of being needed. We both chuckled in unison over sweet nothings. Our love grew with each passing day.

Short were the days, shorter the nights, every hour sped away swiftly like a sail on the sea and under the sail, was an ocean full of treasures, full of joy. Every time when we spoke we weaved a new dream. It was all so pristine. Nivya expressed her fondness and taste for art and handicrafts. She said she would carefully pick crystals, frames, simple elegant pieces of art, crockery, candle stands and paintings while traveling. We imagined a house of our own – vibrant and serene, cozy yet spacious, unconventional and creative, contemporary, organic and green, all of it. We imagined the rooms to have warm colors that would stimulate pleasant conversation between us. Each area and every corner would have its own character. All in all, I knew that our home would be chic – just like her. It would have a beautiful room for Mom and Papa, and besides, there would be a room that would exclusively belong to us. That would be our world, our dream place - where we would have conversations, musings, agreements, arguments, and typical quarrels like couples do. Because, after all said and done, it would be our world, and we would eventually be encircled in each other's arms. Being in each other's arms after a tiff would add so much of meaning to our relationship.

At nights we would hazily find each other sleeping side by side, like spoons, our hands and legs entwined. I would kiss her on the back of her neck and pull her closer in my arms. And each morning, we would be still cuddling. Nivya would wake me up with her soft kisses on my face. And we imagined how I would like to sleep more, lying on my back with my arms around her, and with her face nestled under my chin feeling the smoothness of her breath on my chest.

Such had been our dream, a dream so simple, and so beautiful. So many nights, I woke up, knelt down and prayed for our togetherness. I never knew what exactly to ask for, but it was a mystic state where my consciousness was being absorbed and feelings were getting communicated. Our dream gave sustenance to our souls and it sparked a flame of hope in our hearts.

But the chambers of my heart got out of sync and started beating abnormally. Blood pressure got dangerously high. Minute by minute, reports were being enumerated to know details of all the damages. Surgeons had feverishly punctured every penetrable vein in my body. I had lost more than two pints of blood and was perfectly immobile on the examining table for hours. CT scan had diagnosed a blood clot in one of the brain arteries. They infused me with a clot-busting drug – tissue plasminogen activator, but they couldn't tell if the artery was opening up. It was leading to complexities.

I could feel the energy, the rush. Waking up early in the morning, I would fumble with my pillows to get my hands on my mobile phone to send a good morning message to Nivya. That was my first morning ritual. I would then get fresh and ready, before having breakfast while briefly browsing through newspapers, gulping down a glass of warm milk in successive swigs. I would find my way through the maze of rush hours, and then upon reaching the office I would plough through the accumulated heap of work. There were too many official tasks to complete. Getting a few days leave was difficult. However, I was adamant, as nothing was more important than meeting her. I rushed through things at work.

While months passed by, there was this special month in particular. I wanted to surprise Nivya on her birthday. By then, I had already told Mom about Nivya. She had met Mom once when I got her home. While they were chit chating, I was in the kitchen making tea for all. Mom had already started imagining her as a daughter-in-law. Initially, Nivya used to feel nervous and reluctant to talk to Mom, but gradually it got better. I always knew that she would get along well with all, and that she would get lot of affection from my family.

Mom knew about her birthday, but I was trying to cover it up by making it appear like an official trip. I could have travelled by train and that would have been easy on my pocket. But to avoid time loss I had decided to take the air route. And with private airlines vying with each other with "no frills" marketing gimmicks and with plethora of cost effective choices, I managed to book an air ticket online. I was to board an early morning flight and be back in the evening.

I took a chair to the balcony and sat on it comfortably resting my legs on the parapet. This had become my favorite pastime. As for me all I needed at times was a perfect place for imagination and a sky full of stars to ponder. Again, like a true astronomer I studied the sky trying to understand the intricate patterns. My thoughts traveled of their own volition to her. Meanwhile I also kept a vigil on my watch that was ticking in silence. The moment it struck twelve I called her, but she disconnected. Her parents must have been around. I fail to understand why people find it difficult to wait till the next morning to wish. I too wanted to be the first one to wish her. So I quickly sent here a loved filled birthday message. I waited for her reply, gazing at the stars again letting my mind imagine all sorts of things about her – wondering what she must have been wearing, wondering how she would be missing me, wondering how she would have loved the message that I had sent her. It triggered my imagination of her sight, smell, sound, touch and taste. She called back at around twelve twenty.

She whispered, "Hi Ronnie, sorry love. I was with mom and Papa."

"No worries, baby… I thought so… did you get my message?"

"Yaaaa Ronnie, and I loved it… I must have read it like a hundred times. It is such a lovely message. Thank you so much baby. You make it all so special"

"You are welcome, and here is my kiss to you on your birthday, for your lips… happy birthday", we pouted and kissed over the phone and made those funny sounds.

"I am missing you Ronnie, I wish to be in your arms and I do not like it at all to be so far away from you."

"Me too, you don't know how I've been waiting just to hear your voice. I was getting all crazy."

"Ronnie, I want to celebrate this day with you somehow. I just feel like running away with you somewhere very far. I know you've been trying your best to get an off from work. It was difficult for me as well to make an excuse at home, or else I would have flown to you."

"Do not worry, we are still together. Right now you are in my arms and while you are talking to me, I can feel your breath all over my mouth. I like your fragrance."

"Ronnie! She cried. I miss you."

"Hey, don't cry…"

"You are not here Ronnie… and I don't like anything without you. You know, Papa had got a cake and we just had a kind of small celebration, but while I was cutting the cake and blowing the candle flame, all I could think of was you, you and you. I knew you called and I wanted to grab the phone and answer. But couldn't," she kind of sobbed.

"Ok listen, listen..." I was about to reveal, but I resisted."

In all the excitement to meet her, I hardly slept that night. In the morning, just before boarding the flight, I called up Nivya and told her that I was about to reach Delhi in the next few hours to see her. She squealed in delight. She was aroused and eager to meet me. She said she would rush to the airport to fetch me.

I had worn a smart full sleeves sky blue, checkered shirt, dark blue denim jeans along with a smart jacket. My nerves were bungled up with joy and ecstasy, feeling turtles in my stomach. A different emotion was pulsating through my heart. I got an aisle seat, squishy and warm. Some mid-aged lady, not interested in anything, pale and sleepy, had already occupied the window seat. I settled myself on the seat.

The plane gathered momentum and raced along the runway until it had enough power to lift itself into the sky. The plane's vibration formed the pattern of rhythm of my heart that was constantly beating for Nivya. It was a novel experience of emotions and sensations. I looked around to see the plane gracefully gliding through the sea of spectacular clouds. It was amazing to watch from the crest, floating endless expanse of clouds. Once at cruising altitude, a beautiful air hostess came, "Would you like tea or coffee?" "Coffee of course", I smiled instantly. Her polite and courteous tone was life-infusing. My exhilaration was palpable. Cloud nine was what it was supposed to be and I was on my way to meet my celestial angel, and it all seemed like an embodiment of my romantic dream. To overcome the strange excitement, I closed my eyes, putting on the ear plugs I kept listening to music, covering several miles. And then it was time to fasten the seat belt again as the plane was descending for a gallant landing. The turbulence felt when the wheels crashed on the ground was like a sweet jolt. Other passengers might have found me crazy or something, as I was gleefully smiling at everyone. I felt all the people in the world were so beautiful. Good job Mr. Pilot! Though I felt he needed to learn to fly faster.

My heartbeat was getting trifle fast and I wanted to run to Nivya, but I kept walking steadily with long strides and exalted grove, feeling unusual spring in my steps, craning my neck to see her. With so much of buoyancy, I was swelling with vitality. A surge of adrenaline rushed through my bloodstream. My eyes were searching for her constantly, and I was trying to conceal an inward exultation under a manner of decorous calm. It was making me somewhat nervous as I couldn't get a glimpse of her. I could see so many faces but not the one that I was looking for. I tried calling on her mobile phone but it went unanswered. She wasn't there. I couldn't trace her. It kind of made me nervous for a while.

Just when I reached the exit point, she emerged from behind the barricade and we almost bumped into each other. There she was, to receive me at the airport with a bouquet of freshly picked flowers. I was so happy to see her. She made me feel like a celebrity while she being the most ardent fan in the world, waiting for me. I felt like a suave, swashbuckling hero of a magnum opus!

We reciprocated with broad smiles; hugged each other, and then she gave me those flowers. I found the gesture as sweet as her. Even sweeter was her embrace. I wished it had lasted for some more time. I could see happiness in her smile as she was glowing. The color rose in her cheeks as I held her face and planted the softest kiss on her left cheek. She blushed to crimson tinge. She was wearing a prominent white cotton *salwaar kameez* with *resham* embroidery across the chest, and a matching *duppatta* and *salwaar* with orange hues at the borders. She had then cropped her long hair and they were pulled back firmly and tied at the nape of her neck. Though I preferred her keeping her hair long and open, she was looking beautiful. She told me that it took her a long time to decide on what to wear. You know how girls can be. She had once asked me about my preference and I had told her I would love to see her in a white *salwaar kameez*. And there she was looking beautiful as ever and her smile amenable.

She suggested we go to a restaurant so that we could sit and talk. We went to a 24 hour snack bar at the airport itself. I held out the door open for her to enter. Once inside, we chose to sit as far away from other patrons as possible. Nivya took the bag from my hand and placed it on the opposite chair. We sat next to each other. She took my arm into her lap and held it onto it, putting her hand in mine and rested her hand on my shoulder. We were kind of lost in each other's comfort. It was all so splendid. We were soaking up the regal mystique. After a while, we quietly reminded each other of the need to place an order, lest the waiter started hovering over our heads. I promptly endorsed her suggestion and we ordered for a cheese pizza and some cheese garlic bread. I wasn't actually hungry, as I had croissants which were deliciously fresh, made of layers of tender dough with creamy sweet butter, egg omelet and apple juice on the flight. But I couldn't resist the sight of cheese rich hot pizza. Even the bread that we ate had unique garlic cheese liberally spread over it. We relished it. We then asked for a glass of lemonade topped up with ice cubes. In between all of it, we spoke about family, friends, work and just about all the usual things that we used to talk about. She held my hand in her gentle grip and brought it close to her face. I felt her breath followed by the touch of her soft lips on my thumb. She always maintained that she was fond of my hands for some reason. She said the shape of my fingers and nails indicated of me of being creative and an extremely good lover. It kind of made me raise my eyebrows in delight. I had never thought about that, but I liked what she said.

I studied her palms and fingers. It was all mysterious as I never knew to read fate lines, nor was I sure if anyone can actually determine fate and all by reading palms. Nivya told me that the length, proportion and shape of fingers and hand, indicates information of a person's character. I said, "Ok." And before I could ask what she found about me, she asked me, if I could find my name on her palm. I tried looking at it closely to see a pattern of my name, when she held my index finger and ran the tip of it through the cris-cross of lines on her palm forming alphabets of my name - R O N N I E, to make me realize that my name is her fate, engraved on her palm. That is how we felt for each other. I kissed her palm. Our palms were entwined, caressing each other's fate lines. Her eyes were tenderly whispering me how much she loved me, and mine were replying, 'me too'. We kept looking into each other's eye. I held her hand close to my heart. She never wore a bracelet or bangle or anything metallic, as her soft extremely fair wrists were susceptible to skin reactions. But couple of rings adorned her fingers, and few of them were worn for emotional armor. Nonchalantly, I took a platinum ring out from her ring finger and tried it in my last one and it got stuck mid way. I got the size of her finger. Sliding the ring in her finger back again, I took a sip of lemonade that was lying on the table for quite some time. Nivya wriggled her finger making the ice cubes crinkle in the glass. She made me lick her finger, and then she licked it herself. Yeah … we would do such crazy things at times!

We roamed around the airport for some time, and then remained seated at a quiet end of the airport on a long cushioned bench and talked for long. Somewhere aside from that place, we could hear soft instrumental music being played in the background, with announcements about flights every few minutes. We were nonchalant about the rest of the world. In fact we looked like a couple about to get married, enjoying their courtship. We were at the airport till evening. Amicably we spoke about so many things and were so lost in our conversation.

Then something reminded me. I opened the bag and presented here a polythene bag. It had a soft toy and two dresses which I had picked up from a boutique. I told her how lost I was in that boutique, as I knew nothing about women clothing and how I spent hours just to chose those two dresses. She expressed her delight and liked the dresses. She said she would soon wear them, click snaps and then email them to me. Ironically, I never got to see her wearing them. I am not even sure if she really liked and wore them, or if at all it fitted her properly. I asked her to send the snaps soon so that I could see her wearing them.

Nivya had to appear for an exam the next morning and she said that there was no point in me staying over. I told her I would stay over and will come to fetch her from college after her exam gets over. But she said she won't be able to make any excuse at home to her solicitous parents. So meeting again was not possible. Though wanting me to stay back, she just held my hand and said that we'll meet soon.

I wondered what was wrong with the hour needle in my watch that it ran so fast. Couldn't it just stop then? We were seated on a bench with my jacket on her lap, while we were holding each other's hand. We wanted to spend so much of more time together, but the flight announcement was made. Nivya held my hand and kissed it softy. It was time to leave. She turned towards me, with a glance filled with love. I noticed Nivya calmly looking at me with a palpable feeling, and then she said 'I love you'. I smiled and kissed her hand in return. We were naïve and shy. We were learning.

We got up and moved towards the boarding gate… It had become the most beautiful airport in the world for us. The flowers were carefully placed in my rucksack that I was carrying on my shoulders. We reached the check in counter, and we hugged each other at the same spot where we'd met hours ago, and then were parting way as lovers do. She was in my embrace as I held her close to me. I released her gently from my arms. I felt hollow inside to move away from that spot. Slowly, I walked past the security gate and then turned back to look at her waiving at me. I could see her moist eyes. My spontaneous impulse was to run and grab her there and then, but...

The sun had set and the dark sky absorbed the orange hue. I was on my flight back to my city. This time when I boarded the flight,

I prayed in silence for our well being, closed my eyes and caught a wonderful cat-nap.

When I reached back, I decided to buy a diamond ring for Nivya, as I thought of it being a wonderful symbol of commitment and love and all that. I had her ring size. I was a novice when I decided to take the plunge to buy my first diamond ring. Since I was buying it for the first time, I tried to learn a few things about it and inquired from various possible sources. I took Sanjana's help, and I had to tell her about Nivya. Sanjana happily agreed to come along with me to find the ring.

She took me to an exquisite showroom known to her. I browsed through so many of them displayed on the counter and my untrained eye caught a glimpse of an enticingly glistening ring which was a real crystal marvel. I saw the price tag only to feel a sweet jolt, but then it was priceless and beautiful. The choice was made. I bought it home and carefully kept the small box in a safe place known to me.

It was meant as a surprise for Nivya. It was a dream that I had nurtured about the day when I would take her beautiful hand in mine - gently I would hold the most beautiful hand I had ever known and slide the ring in her tender, beautiful finger and kiss it.

We had not imagined we would meet so soon. Just about a month had gone by and she was there to receive me at the railway station. She was getting more beautiful with each passing day. Public places don't give you a chance to meet unrestrained. So a big smile, a side hug and a slight peck on her cheek, and we came out of the station towards the auto stand. I loved the way she negotiated the fare, and I was quite impressed at the way she had adapted herself in an unfamiliar city. We went to Defense Colony where we hung around for some time and then decided to go to Barista to sip some hot coffee. I was there for a week and we had a chance to meet daily. The plan was perfect. Nivya had enrolled herself for some trivial computer graphics crash course in a local institute, which meant that she could bunk it for the entire week. The best part was that the key trainer in the institute was Nivya's very good friend, so all was set. Def Col became our meeting point where we would daily meet at 11.00 am and then we would go places only to be back by 3.00 pm. Trust me, those few hours were too less. We did not even realize how fast time sped away. I told you sometimes I had a problem with the hour needle.

Scampering through similar looking roads and by-roads of Delhi left me with no sense of route. Stopping and asking for directions, I would manage to reach the institute and call her. She used to come down in almost a flash. We hugged each other and she felt extremely shy. We decided to leave that place quickly. Nivya had bought her scooty. When she started it, I batted my lashes at her a couple of times before I sat behind her. I held on to her wrapping my hands around her waist while she rode. It was a ride of our lifetime. We sang a love song, while she was gracefully maneuvering through twists and turns and through tree lined streets of Def Col. It was all so surreal and dreamlike. She could feel my breath on the nape of her back and felt funny. I gently kissed the back of her neck. She almost lost her balance as it sent a pleasant shiver down her spine. She giggled and told me to stop it. I just held her close in my arms and closed my eyes resting my face on the back of her shoulder, while other cars and two wheelers whizzed past us. We rode at our own pace. She was worried if someone saw us like that, but then not many knew us in the city. The reverie broke when the scooty came to a halt. We reached the destination.

Each day, we went to different places like *Ansal Plaza, Lajpat Nagar,* and *Connaught Place*, strolling through the sprawling concentric and fashionable market place, replete with imperial Victorian architect, plethora of shops, spick and span restaurants, fast-food joints and clustered outlets of almost all leading international brands in colonnaded white buildings. We strolled all around holding each other's hands.

Later we did some shopping, and Nivya helped me in selecting a mauve color dress for Roshni from one of the known places and the name that I could not even recall later. The entire week got over and I was back home, and it all happened so quickly.

Roshni liked the color and pattern, and she asked me how I selected that particular color. I told her it was Nivya's choice so it was bound to be good. She said, "Yeah, why not?" Roshni got a call on her mobile and she disconnected. She got a call again. I asked her who was calling as it was quite late in the evening. I took the mobile from her hand and saw Abhi's name flashing.

He had been one moron who always got over my nerves. How could Roshni be in love with such a dork? I hated Abhi when I saw him for the first time. When I met him, I saw that his eyes were mild and genial telling me to accept him, and his voice was low and kind. "Stay away from Roshni", I said. He hesitantly asked me the reason. If I would have had a gun, I would have shot him there and then between his eyes. I gave him a stare that would have scared the shit out of him. I told him that I was not there to answer to his questions. I spoke to him in a manner, something in a way that my Papa would have said, "You guys are too young to indulge in things like love and marriage. Better! You take up your career seriously and stay away from this nonsense …" I raised one of my eyebrows with my index finger warning him to keep away! Abhi being two inches taller than me had his head bowed down. I clearly indicated that I would never ever let him be a part of our family. Perhaps, I was too presumptuous. I guess Roshni was expecting something altogether different from me. We both in a way were disappointed and uncomfortable with each other. So we stopped talking to each other for a while.

For quite some time, my instincts told me that there was something wrong and my premonitions were series of some outrageous thoughts. We had not spoken for more than two weeks. And it felt like ages to me. If not in the day time, Nivya would usually call up in the middle of the night when her parents were asleep. But then, it was for the first time that we could not contact each other for a very long period. Whenever I tried calling on her mobile it went unanswered or got disconnected. I would sit on the cliff overlooking the empty sky and nurse surging emotions. It was like an endless loop hovering above. The sky looked hollow, not in the cosmic sense, but real sense, void and vague. Many nights passed by.

I kept waiting for my mobile to ring, and every time it rang or I got a message, my heart missed a beat only to realize that it was from someone else. Even more frustrating was to get those unsolicited and utter nuisance messages, trying to sell some cheesy dial tunes and holiday packages in the dead of the night. I felt like throwing my mobile out of the window, but somehow I maintained my sanity. I would just keep it near my pillow while sleeping so that I could never miss her call or message. I waited. And my heart kept vibrating in silent mode.

Something was wrong somewhere, I thought. Every time we spoke, I could sense that there was something that was bothering Nivya. I was apprehended in strange feelings that were clamoring my mind. Initially, I thought things would be alright, but it wasn't getting any better. She evaded if I tried to ask. I wasn't able to gauge what she was expecting. She would pour out questions at me that would annoy me. 'What if one day I came to know that she was in love with someone else?' It triggered an unexpected reaction, as if I had tripped over a landmine of emotion. It made me furious. For some reason I did not even like the thought of it, even if it was intended for finding my reaction. What should have been my answer! My instincts answered her, maybe in an unusual way. I told her that I would kill her...

It was harsh and I felt a lump in my throat when I said that. I was angry. She was aghast by my reply and realized how bad I felt. There was some kind of unpleasantness in the air, a pervading harshness that hadn't been there before. The silence was awkward. This was not the way I ever spoke to her. She had put a hypothetical situation, perhaps, to know my reaction. There was long confounded silence between us. I knew I was rude and I should have not said that. I kept thinking about it later, and her question kept nagging my mind. Those raft of words and impulsive thoughts kept me awake.

My family too had not slept for nights at stretch. There was very little that could have been done to reverse the initial brain damage caused by trauma. There were no cognitive response and no vital signs of my reflexes, when accessing my level of consciousness. I could still not open my eyes. The emergency department's primary concern was to make sure that I was getting proper oxygen supply to the brain and rest of my body, maintaining adequate blood flow and controlling my blood pressure. As soon as these things were being worked on, my almost dead body was taken for some neurological examination. My body temperature, pulse and breathing rate, pupil size in response to light were checked, and it all seemed dreadful. I was hooked on to a ventilator since my vital organs were severely damaged. I was sedated and incubated. There was no hope of survival. Doctors were in dilemma to continue with the life support as it would prove detrimental by causing pain and prolonging the dying process. Papa never wanted to take a chance. He told doctors to not worry about money as he would have put everything at stake, and done everything possible. I was put on life support system and that did not mitigate suffering, it only added to the agony. Situation was getting worse, and the anxiety crept frustration, while everyone was expecting a miracle.

This was also some kind of a miracle, somewhere in late May. It was hot and humid, as eight rainless months had passed. We were all whizzing through our lives, and for a while each of us got caught up in our own world. I had no clue then, that after meeting Nivya in Delhi, it would take us ages to meet again. We were waiting for our time. We were missing each other like crazy. We had spent endless hours and hours talking to each other over the phone. To an extent that it did make us feel so close to each other, but being together was a different thing. Seeing each other, holding hands, touching and kissing each other, eating and roaming together brings in so much of joy and we were missing all of that.

The epicenter of my happiness pulsated in rhythm and I was jumping all over the place in excitement. Suddenly I was lively, vivacious and bouncy. I was hopping like a goat in glee on eating those berries. I hugged Karan tightly and cackled. She had called me up and had given a pleasant surprise. She was coming to Mumbai for a day. She had a wedding to attend somewhere in Pune. And she told me we might get some time to spend together. But there was a hitch. She was coming with her parents.

How could a day be just good enough for us, when we wanted to spend our entire life together! Here it was not even a day… only a couple of hours. But then we had been waiting for this. All the months that went by, we had somehow maintained our sanity. That had required a lot of positive mental conditioning. But after we got to know that we were about to meet, each passing moment had become more difficult to pass by. We spoke for long, with so much of enthusiasm. We wanted to hug and kiss each other. It was all further building up the excitement. And in that sheer exhilaration she cautioned me that her parents should not even get the faintest of clue about anything of that sort… But my joy knew no bounds. Rain began to plummet in drizzle.

She reached Mumbai with her parents. They were put up in Churchgate in some government guest house. She called up and gave me the address. I drove my car all the way, with full throttle, all enthused to meet her with my heart springing in joy, all along listening to peppy songs I had loved the most. I reached well before time and had to wait outside the guest house for more than an hour. We kept texting each other. She was constantly plotting to find a way and sneak away from her terminally conservative parents. I got down from the car and to make rounds near the guest house to check if I could get a glimpse of her. I kept waiting, kicking around. She was so close yet beyond sight. The watchman at the gate felt somewhat suspicious and might have been wondering what I was up to. I guess I had become an incurable romantic.

Nivya finally got a chance to move out, on a pretext of buying some books from the fountain area. And when I saw her coming out of the gate, I quickly reached my car to start it and opened the door for her. There she was, almost out of breath, and in that excitement, we hugged each other, followed by a confused kiss – somewhere near the cheeks and lips. We laughed. She had put on some flab but was looking fab as ever in a white sleeveless *kurti* and light blue jeans. There was such a charm and softness in her manner that never failed to allure me. She said that we had only half an hour. That was heartbreaking – half an hour ONLY. We wanted to talk about so many things and spend so much of time together. She was thinking about the ways I could be introduced to her parents. We could not come up with any good idea so we postponed the idea of me meeting her parents for sometime later. She said she will have to buy some books. We had so less time. But I guess that was the way it was supposed to be then. So, while we drove, we spoke about so many things in random. We stopped next to a vendor selling books by the pavement. There were random pedestrians and motor traffic. Quickly, we got down, and she purchased a couple of books without even bothering to check the content. No negotiations, quick buy, and we were in the car again. She got a call from her mom and she informed she was on her way back. I realized it was sheer pestering. We reached the guest house. That half an hour got over in no time, and the meeting ended in a confused kiss again. She wanted to kiss me more but was scared someone might see. While I looked into her eye with intensity, she touched my cheeks and whispered, 'see you soon… love.' My eyes were continuously glued on to her while she got down from the car and walked hurriedly to the guest house, a few meters away. Oh! I realized she forgot the books on the dashboard. I remained in the car, looking at the gate, waiting, as I hoped she might just come back. But then she was with her family, probably trying to explain to them what she did in the last half an hour. I took the books wrapped in a polythene bag, and wondered who would read them. They had to leave for Pune the same evening. While driving back home I kept thinking about her and only her, with such fixation. The songs that I played were not peppy anymore; they were soft, melancholic tunes. We were away from each other again.

All night, I tossed and turned, struggled with my pillow on the bed. Then eventually after much of struggle I could get some sleep. I would try to think positive and remain cheerful. There were mixed feelings. I would forget about food, will not be able to sleep, and found that nothing really mattered except being with her. And the fact that Nivya was away from me made it all so unbearable. But our hope to be together again kept us going. Slowly, as time passed by, our length of conversations over the phone got shorter and distance kept growing.

Dawn would find me dejected. But in hope, I would begin my day doing routine things. When I reached office, I could see slew of unattended papers strewn across my desk. I would work all day in the office trying to meet deadlines, sales target, sitting in board meetings, listening to things I never wanted to listen to. And the day would come to an end somehow.

I would reach home exhausted after a grueling day, thinking that I would sleep the moment I hit the bed. And all I would do is find myself fitfully tossing and turning around. God! What had happened to me? I had lost my sleep. I would try to spend time by listening to music or reading a book. I'd never been an avid reader. The lazy me, always preferred watching movies or surfing the internet in my free time. But there was this book in particular out of the three that Nivya had bought the other day. It was about how to achieve impossible dreams. I read a couple of pages and then dozed off. Though the book was sleep inducing, I never gave up. I kept reading more and more pages. And then I realized that I'd been reading it diligently for quite a few nights and the subject would keep drifting whimsically. The book was about how to realize your dream, and the good thing it did was that it stimulated me in catching up with sleep and that too, a dreamless sleep! With eyes closed and that book on my chest, this fool would retire.

Each and every day, intriguing moments crossed my path - some notions and some observations. I was witnessing and feeling the chaotic molecules inhabiting our world. One day, I was parking my bike while Roshni was crossing the road to enter a mall, an obnoxious drunk laggard made a pass at her and misbehaved. He was unaware that big brother was with her. A flurry of fists and bone-crunching knocks and the next moment that guy was writhing on the ground grousing. No words were exchanged and I had thrashed the living daylights out of him. One day, I lost my mobile phone. It slipped from my hands and fell in the commode. I made it a point to never talk over the phone in the toilet. I bought a new handset which in itself was quite a task, with so many options available. One day I met Karan and we spent an hour or so enthusing and planning about the joys of bike riding and going on an excursion. We went to the beach in his car and bought some really chilled beer cans. Parking his big car along the boulevard, we sipped chilled beer gingerly, gazing at the stars in the sky. One day, surprisingly I reached the office early. After work, I would stroll alone in the evening for long. One day I fretted all day with a melody in my head, trying to figure out where it originated from but in vain. Since I liked it, I hummed along. One day I went for a company party where a nice mix of people turned up to network, while some showed up to with an intention of getting drunk enough to say things to fellow cubicle mates they never had balls to say on a regular work day. It was the first time I tried black cherry infused vodka – 'Black Forest Martini'. One day, I took Mom and Roshni for a movie and then lunch. I also wanted to break the ice with Roshni. Movie was good and so was lunch, so later I sportingly agreed to join them on their desultory shopping spree. The extravagant mall, teeming with shoppers had just about everything under the sun, but I felt too bored to buy anything. So I roamed around enlightening myself with latest trends and checking some hottest mobile phones and laptops, while Mom and Roshni did their shopping for footwear and dresses in snazzy boutiques. There were people everywhere with shopping bags, I noticed that some girls had colored their hair with shades of streaky burgundy while some sported bold purple. Fashion was catching up with jeans getting tighter and lower by the waist showing pierced belly which had become a true embodiment of being trendy. One day, Karan was back in the city after his short trip to London. Again, we took two beers and went in the car to the beach when the sun had set. We discussed various ideas, had long conversations about our hopes and our philosophical discussions. And then we also planned for Mohit's wedding. All of us got a chance to meet after a long time. We had a great time during Mohit's marriage and all of us enjoyed it to the hilt. Days just passed by. Some days were different, while some monotonous, hopelessly long winded and repetitive. And all the while I kept missing Nivya. The song that touched my nerve in those days was unchained melody. I would keep singing and listening to that song... God speed your love to me ...

Days passed into weeks and weeks drifted into silent and difficult months with moments of truth and love, flickering and fading in my mind. I saw some of my friends and cousins getting married and settling down. I smiled and congratulated them, but inside I was eating my heart out. I had started saving money in different forms of investments, and was careful not to splurge unnecessarily. Yet, at the end of months, bills would pile up and I paid all the hard earned money for common and unavoidable trappings. It was ok, as I considered it to be just money that I could earn back anytime. But I had to start thinking about my future seriously. Nivya was constantly worried with what was happening at her home and between her parents. She was getting insecure. I was unable to understand the intricacies of the matter and we were having tiffs and arguments over trivial things. Nivya would remain disturbed because of her parent's persistent assertion of getting married to someone.

Whenever, thinking about Nivya, I was acutely aware of the differences in our respective upbringings. She was delicately bought up in wealthy surroundings, with servants, drivers and other amenities that are generally considered luxuries. On the other hand, I came from a modest background, imbibing middle-class values with no qualms about it. Our family always had a simple life, but never an austere one. We got the best of everything. But Nivya's parents would have not been keen on the young man, whom their daughter had taken a shine to.

Being the only child, she had always been a cynosure of her parent's eyes. Nivya told me that her parents had very high expectations. So what? I always had high aspirations in life. That thought never deterred me in following a dream we both cherished, for love was something where our imagination was taking precedence over intelligence. Why won't her parents like me? I couldn't pin down the reason. I suspected that their prejudices were legion. Her staunchly religious mother, coming from an inhibited background wanted her daughter to marry someone from their own community. Get real! Is what I would say. There had never been a perfect wedding and there would never be one. That thought came to my mind inherently. Nivya was afraid to reveal about us to them because of the fear to lose me forever. I guess her parents had always been chronically unreasonable. She said her mother would never approve her of being in a relationship and would tear my photograph if shown to her. I told her not to worry, as my photographs were not that bad and I had them in plenty. But seriously speaking, Nivya used to get somber and anxious, thinking all about it. Her parents must have had their wishes known to her, but forgot to ask her what she preferred.

Nivya had no issues with what I was doing and had no apprehensions whatsoever. And that was one of my strengths. The reason I had gained so much of confidence in pursuing our marriage was because of her faith in me. At that time, I was struggling with my career and not had enough money to spend lavishly. I could not afford a luxurious car and treatment, nor could I buy her expensive gifts. She always understood that. She never made me feel embarrassed or small about it. Even if I ever tried to raise the topic, she would gently put it away. Nivya would never talk about money with me. Once in a while, out of concern, she would ask me about my work and if everything was fine.

Nivya never craved for worldly things and never bothered for materialistic pleasure. At times she paid for our restaurant bills, not allowing me to do so. It pinched me, because she had not yet started earning and it was her Papa's money. So I made my sweetheart realize it, and never allowed her to get money out of her purse again. I think she liked me for it.

Though she wasn't overtly traditional, she always gave importance to faith, prayer and patience. She wanted to pursue her career for some time after marriage, before going the family way. She was always extremely fond of kids and experiencing motherhood was her deeply cherished and profound desire.

Nivya never wanted to marry a doctor or an engineer for reasons known to her. I too, never cared to ask her the reason. But her parents wanted her to marry a doctor or an engineer, with high degree of perfection, preferably settled abroad. It would be an added advantage if the boy or his parents were American citizens. Now it was too late, and there was no way that I could've actually become a doctor or an engineer. Yeah! I actually thought of impersonating myself to be a doctor, and then getting married to her and then may be later we could have revealed the truth – the way it happens in movies and all. But then I wanted to be accepted for what I was, and I could not come up with any better thought.

Nivya had a different idea altogether. She said that we would have to make it all look like an arranged marriage. So we started thinking about cooking and spicing up a nice and believable story. Since she knew her parents well and had a plan, not convincing though, I was ready for execution, anytime. I believed with time she would find the courage to reveal it to her parents and confront them, though I had started to wonder if our family would ever get along well.

I had to get my priorities right. All this while I had just wanted one thing from her but never wanted to compel her for a promise. And one day I got to hear something that I was waiting for. She told me that she just belonged to me and no one else, and no matter what; she would come to me in any situation. My parents would have accepted Nivya without any shilly-shallying. The problem was with her parents in accepting me.

She wished to travel the world but never wanted to settle abroad, simply because she never wanted to be away from her parents. Being the only daughter, I knew how important parents were for her. I never wanted her to elope, as it would have had hurt her parents' pride and sentiments. But only if time demanded and if situation worsened, we would have taken some drastic decision, accordingly. We were prepared to survive her parent's opposition and be together under any circumstances. She once mentioned that we were together for eternity, or practically speaking, till death did us apart. We trusted each other completely. I loved her for all her feelings for our relationship and it made me feel so strong that she trusted me so much. Our dreams never ceased. We spent countless nights working with our dreams, triggering a flood of images and emotions that swept us off our feet. We knew marriage meant lots of responsibilities and attention. I had to do well in my career. I had to rise to the occasion and prove myself. There was so less time, and so much to do. Although I was not daunted by the thought, I knew I could not afford to be complacent about it. The stage was set, motivation was high and I had to deliver.

One day in my office, I saw a concealed envelope lying on my desk with my name written on it. I tore the envelope carefully by the side to uncover an invitation. Only two of us from our department were invited. I had told Nivedita that as soon as I would get promoted I would talk to our parents about our marriage. I picked the best suit from my wardrobe, and a designer silk tie that I had recently bought. Well I just had two suits, and to pick the best didn't really take much. I whisked an extra dash of hair gel. It was a company's party where some major and important announcements were to be made. We had some delegates coming from Hong Kong. Mayank and I were the chosen ones amongst other colleagues for this particular event. We were quite excited about it. It was something that actually did not come to us as a surprise, as we were anticipating a new branch to come up in Bangalore and the choice for heading the process was obvious. Towards the end of some presentations and announcement, couple of papers in the envelopes, were discreetly thrust into our hands by our senior manager. It was kind of building up the suspense. The moment I read the letter, an electric tremor of anxiety quivered through me like a thunderbolt. It was a pink slip with two months compensation cheque. The recession period in our company had forced the authorities to blow away a few chunks of workforce like straws in wind flurry. And to soften the blow, the human resource people had come with this innovative idea of a 'Five Star Lay off'. I was quixotically frozen. I felt as if thousands of devils were conspiring against me. There was literally a time when the company could not do anything without my involvement. And after all the efforts and commitment that I had put in, I was being courteously asked to leave. It was a jolt that moved me from my core. There was a strange feeling the next day when I entered the office for signing exit papers. The floor was abuzz with low hum of computers keyboards clanking, ringing phones and people scrambling across. My friends and colleagues with whom I shared my cubicle were shocked to hear the news. There was palpable anxiety in the air. It was a big setback. No questions were asked, no emotions were involved.

I was not sure how I would reveal it to Nivya. It was already late. By then I should have had already put the marriage proposition in front of her parents. I felt very uneasy to talk about it to anyone. But I spoke to Nivya about it as I used to share everything with her. I did not tell my parents and Roshni that I was asked to put down my papers in the office. I just made them to believe that I wasn't happy with the job and needed a change. Nivya encouraged me to not to lose heart as she believed something better would come out of it. She asked me to not take it too personally as even the best of the best are not immune to layoffs. Finding a new job was not an issue. 'Head hunters' came to my rescue. It took two weeks or so before I got another job in a better organization with a 30% hike. So yes, Nivya was right. The layoff turned out to be a blessing in disguise – something better had happened. And yes I started believing that everything happens for a reason and everything happens for good. Right intention and right efforts would always bring out the best.

But then all the efforts had been made, but I showed no discernible signs of improvement. It became worst. There were absolutely no reflexes that I showed. It indicated a profound level of coma. Doctors who were trying to revive me pointed out that eyes, bone and heart valves could be donated up to 24 hours after death. Donation of body organs could be considered only after death, after the brain ceases to function. The artificial support system was maintaining oxygenation of my organs, and transplanting those organs could help terminally ill patients. Instead of getting charred, the organs could give a new lease of life to someone. The hospital authorities asked Papa if he would fill a prescribed consent form. He could just not believe what he heard. He got furious, but then he was helpless. He pleaded with them to not give up.

We had developed this never say die attitude. No matter what circumstances came our way, we surmounted it and faced all the challenges head on. It had been a few hectic years for Nivya as well. She did exceptionally well for herself to pass with exceeding grades. Her family was happy and proud of her achievement. After her semesters, she started with her internship. Nivya felt she had a lot of ground to cover on the home front, career, and mainly her scholarship applications. She was expecting a scholarship in the US, but told me that since I was here, she would not consider it.

She kept telling me she needed to discuss something important with me for quite some time. I could feel the strained anxiety that had gripped her, in her voice. I kept asking for it but she kept postponing as she wanted the right time for it. She said it would be better if we did not speak about it on the phone and only when we met. Meeting her for next one month was not possible. I was curious. She said she would call me late in the night and talk about it. Late till the dead of night, I kept waiting but she did not call.

I waited for nights after nights and I did not get her call. When I tried, her phone was engaged, unanswered or switched off. It was all getting so annoying.

She finally called

Hi

Hi Ronnie, how are you?

I am ok. How about you?

Not ok. I am in a big trouble. She sounded to be in a rush and overtly worried.

What happened?

I'll tell you everything. But you will have to listen to it all very carefully. And please for God's sake don't derive any conclusions.

Ok, but what is it?

Listen, I am in Dehradun, at one of our relative's place. Mom, Papa and everyone else are in the next room, so if anyone comes, I might just hang up. I'll call you as and when I can, so you don't call me as I won't be able to take your call. I may even land up in big trouble.

But…

Listen… someone's here … I'll have to cut the call. Bye for now. Love you.

She hung up the call.

The suspense was building up, as I knew it was something serious. I did not even know how to elaborate all the incidences that happened. All the information that I got were based on scattered bits and pieces, not completing the entire picture. Nivya told me that her parents had liked someone based in the US, and her marriage was secretly fixed by them. All the relatives invited from both the sides had come to attend their engagement and other ceremonies. All this had happened in a very short notice without Nivya being aware of it. It was one of the most appalling jolts that had manifested over me.

What crap? How could anything like that happen? I asked myself. How could a girl and guy get married without each other's consent? Everything seemed so strange. The feelings were mixed – I was a bit shocked, a bit pissed off, and a bit apprehensive. But I listened to her as she spoke.

She told me that she could not deny the guy outright; hence meeting that 'someone' was important, or else her parents would have realized that there was something wrong. I felt a twinge of annoyance. Her neurotic parents had actually fixed her marriage with some doctor from the US. Not once, but she had met the guy a couple of times. She avoided informing me, as she felt it would unnecessary burden me. When she met this doctor, she hinted him about me, and told him clearly that she would not want to get married to him. She also asked him to reject her for some reason. But instead, the doctor started liking her and wanted to marry her.

His name was 'Sartaj', who seemed to be a nice guy, well settled and the only son, who did his doctorate from Delhi and then went to the US where he had started practicing and now wanted to marry someone from India and settle abroad for life. She had met his family as well and they had liked her. I couldn't camouflage my feelings, I was doomed with envy. 'Why do I have to know so much about him?' I was apathetically interested in how she felt about him and his family. I asked her why she even met him in the first place. My expressions were impassive, but anger bestowed me. I wasn't really trying to make a mountain of a molehill. What I disliked the most was the poor communication that we had over such a big episode.

For the first time, we had a long and heated argument. It was quite disturbing. May be I was being overly sensitive, and over reacting. She said she did not like it, when I suspected so much. I was consciously aware that I could not appear to be a chauvinist, and had to handle it carefully to not let things blow out of proportion, or else we would have lost it all. Whatever the answer may be, it required my thoughtful engagement. It required me to be very clear about my real values and to act upon them. I was aware that being overbearing and suspicious could destroy a beautiful relationship. I told her I just needed to know what all exactly happened.

Many men had tried to woo her but she had refused them all. Nivya persistently kept receiving numerous proposals from many eligible bachelors belonging to well-to-do and influential families. All this had started while she was still in college. Her parents too wanted to arrange her marriage in time, but she was adamant. She did not succumb to her parents' plea. She had already made up her mind to not marry until she completed her studies. Her father failed to persuade her. Her relatives soon joined the bandwagon, and spoke to her gently. "You may continue to pursue your studies, even after marriage, as long as you wish to, but do not reject a proposal from such a good family. We understand that you are young and would want to get married to someone you are sure about. So take your time, but at least meet the family. Don't make a decision that might compel you to regret later."

Nivya could not perhaps find a suitable excuse. She felt it was not the correct time to reveal about me. Even if she had mustered courage to tell her parents about me, it would have backfired, as love marriage was considered to be impious in her family.

Nivya's mind was getting torn apart with conflicting thoughts. She decided to meet Sartaj. I am not sure about the exactness, but these were just some of my vague, sparse and poignant imagination. When Nivya meet him, she asked him to reject the proposition point blank. That would not leave any doubts in her parent's mind. I wasn't even sure if any photographs were exchanged before they actually met, but several horoscope papers were consulted and Sartaj was considered a good match. Nonsense is not the word for it, and that is what I felt without any outlandish exaggeration. I decided to avoid the topic on astrology matters, rather than invoking any futile debate – as it can get so phony, to know that every facet of our daily lives and future depends upon the position of celestial bodies commuting its mysterious course thousands of millions of miles away. Ok fine! I loved looking at the stars sparkling in the sky but that was about it. My so called intelligence told me that astrology had no real significance, and nothing else mattered when there is true love.

The phone got disconnected again. I imagined how Nivya must have met Sartaj and how she must have been forced to present herself. I was not even sure what all went between the families. All the thoughts were defeating and I felt I was losing everything. I wondered what could stop her from calling me and sending me messages on my mobile for so long. How much did Sartaj know about me? What was happening? Was Nivya getting engaged? Damn! I felt so insecure. I knew I had to stop speculating as all my queries would have got answered. I had to keep my cool. Patience was the key. As I needed a breath of fresh air, I went for a short walk.

I had not hidden my feelings for her from anyone. But the secrecy that she had maintained was proving to be detrimental. Clandestine relationships can get crazy as it leads to stress and frustration. She always confided her feelings to me. Although she feared reprisal and disapproval from her family, she was trying best on her part to not let things slip away. No matter how hard I tried to stay positive, negative thoughts kept creeping in. The mere thought of separation was extremely unpleasant. That was the first time I felt a sting of tears in my eyes. Being in love was bond to bring tears sooner or later. I never knew what would happen to us, to our cloaked romance.

When she called up again, we spoke for a long time. The conversation was not really heading in a specific direction. I had a bag full of questions. And as she was answering my unending questions, she asked me with a bit of annoyance, "Do you believe in me?"

I said, "Of course, I believe in you. Because... I love you."

There was silence. It allowed us to gather our thoughts.

That statement made so much sense – to both of us. As if, it explained everything. It released all the confusion and uncertainty. She cried and reciprocated her feelings for me.

She wasn't bitter with me, I realized at once. She had become more determined. I recognized the difference immediately. She was not petulant, but strong-minded.

Love had changed our lives. Overflowing desire was burning.

Nivy'a parents believed that the girls needed to learn the art of making home attractive the most – as girls aren't supposed to make career choices. Conventionally and genetically, they are designed to deliver babies and take care of family. That is what girls are supposed to do – nurture. It all turned out to be an embarrassment for them. She denied getting married to a guy her parents were keen on. They were shocked at the audacity of their daughter who had been docile all along, to go against their wish. Tongues of so many meddlesome relatives that are always portent and worthless forms without any substance kept accusing and criticizing her. She became a victim of over exaggerated allegations, and her environment did not foster healthy interaction. She found herself caught between helpless circumstance and emotional influence. Her mother's howling torched her and her father's pleading hollowed her heart. The barbs and brickbats that she faced kept getting murkier and dense. Her situation within her own home became hostile, she could not bear it and it all took a toll over her health.

Her parents felt she created a mockery and bought disgrace to their family by going against them to break the marriage irretrievably, that too, for no apparent reason explained. I never knew that all that episodes would have had such an effect on her. Nivya suffered a nervous breakdown and had a brush with serious illness. She was on antidepressants.

I felt it was my responsibility to salvage the situation somehow. The courage she had shown was to be reciprocated. Love did its magic and it bought back hopes that were in turmoil for some time. I knew it was not the time to sit back and brood, but to take action.

The remedy was not antidepressant, but my presence that would have given her comfort. She told me she needed me badly, and the courage to perceive the inconceivable was born out of nowhere.

Nivya wanted her parents to be happy with her choice, and she wanted it to happen the right way. So I had to do settle down with my career, have my parents to talk to her parents and make everything look like it was all arranged. But the distance between us was proving to be difficult as it prevented us from communicating properly. One missed call from her, one text, one simple message, one call, one off-line, one email, was all it would have taken to warm me to my very core. But it did not happen. There were a few misunderstandings that had cropped up between us. We were kind of annoyed with each other. She said it was over and would never talk to me.

I made numerous calls. But Bell's invention, that had made so much advancement in technology over the years, failed to yield her voice. She would not attend my calls nor respond to my messages. My emails were not replied. I started hating the internet. A month passed by and I thought she would eventually get over with her anger.

It was driving me crazy. I wanted to know what exactly was reeling on in her mind. I was loaded with so much of work and was dying to meet her. I wanted to break away that vicious circle of misinterpretation, assumptions and silence.

It was time for me to fly to Delhi. This time I wanted to clear all the confusion and make her realize that her misunderstanding was nothing but bad comprehension. In my entire journey I was constantly thinking about her and if she would be able to meet me. I envisaged many possibilities - to barge in at her place of work, showing up unannounced, and if needed, at home to confront her parents and tell them that we love each other. I was mustering courage as it was time to face the consequence. I may have been frowning or something because the air hostess did not serve me water in spite of me asking it twice. I was too shy to ask for it again, and then I got more occupied in thinking of all the odd possibilities that could happen as I made up immense array of scenarios in my mind. May be I won't be able to talk to Nivya or meet her at all. May be she would deny in front of her parents that she even knows me. May be she would just cling on to me and cry. It was a whimsical journey of improbable dimension. In a matter of few hours I was in a different city. I had no clue Delhi could be so cold in mid February. It was late in the evening and I literally froze on my way from airport to the hotel.

I wasn't carrying any warm clothes with me. I had two days of stay, and they were a living hell. I was constantly trying to call her on her mobile and home phone number which was always engaged, unanswered or switched off. Those were horrendous nights and I could not sleep or relax at all. I was going crazy with tormenting questions and constant battle with my self esteem. She had mysteriously disappeared from my life, all so sudden. Clueless, I roamed in the city of strangers in search of her, letting my gaze drift to places where we'd been together. Saddened, I reflected upon happier times. It brought back all memories of our togetherness. I sent her a text message "im in delhi. plz tke my call".

Finally, my phone vibrated, a text message was received, "im not in delhi … will reach late in the evening … why did u do this to me … im terribly hurt."

I was dejected to know she was not in the city and she felt that I had done something wrong. She was disillusioned, and I had to do everything and anything to make her feel better and come out of that state of mind. But the fact that she wasn't there in the city also meant that I would have had to travel back to Mumbai without meeting her. Two days had passed by and I had a flight to catch the next morning. I felt a strong craving and unsettling unrest within me. Weird thoughts were getting fluent inside my head. I wouldn't call it suffering, but those moments were full of anxieties. Suffering was a matter of choice, and I had denied it. All I knew was I had to get in contact with her somehow, to proclaim our love. I was brimming with unusual energy and uncontrollable restlessness. There was undying strength in me, to go through all hardships to get her. I messaged her again, "can we meet?" Her reply, "not in the evening … but may be tomorrow morning … will call u once I reach home." Her message gave me somewhat relief as at least she was finally responding and was open to the idea of meeting. That was just so important.

Every minute till evening that passed, was in anticipation of her message or call. My mind that had kept buzzing with all the what-ifs, mellowed down. I went to a coffee shop and asked for a hot cup of refreshing coffee. It didn't seem too strong, but frothy and creamy. As I stirred some brown sugar, and drew the cup close to my nose, the smell of the steaming coffee warmed my soul; I began to see my surroundings with different eyes. It made me relax a bit. And while I was having coffee, Nivya called up. I loved coffee.

We were to meet in Connaught Place (CP) the next morning. I cancelled my ticket. Nivya had got a chance to be with her dad for half an hour or so. That wasn't much of time, but we would somehow manage to talk for a few minutes. If not, we would at least get a glimpse of each other. It was worth it, but I got hopelessly stuck in the morning snarling traffic of Delhi while coming from Noida where I was staying at my cousin's place. There was perfect chaos and because of perpetual honking, I could barely hear Nivya's voice on the phone. It was damn irritating. I despise people honking like crazy. I kept pestering the auto rickshaw guy to break all the rules, telling him to keep moving - dodge fast and overtake whatever came in the way. I normally despise people breaking traffic rules, but I had no other option but to let other people despise me on that particular day. We got gridlocked due to a procession on the road. The driver was also kind of fed up of me and my restlessness. Even he felt relieved when we finally reached. Happier he must have been as I did not care to tender exact change, and left a big note. Then I realized how big CP is.

I dangerously crossed the road with fast moving vehicles. While darting forward, I almost collided with a man crossing the road from the opposite side. The man shouted angrily, muttering local expletives under his breath. "Sorry". I was in hurry. Nivya gave me directions on mobile. We had decided to meet at Mc Donald's, but I reached the wrong one. I realized that this one in particular was supposed to be in the inner circle. I just kept running, only to stop and ask for directions, while still talking to Nivya over the phone. She kept asking me where I was, and I kept telling her about it, but both of us were utterly clueless. She said her Papa would soon be back and thus she might have to just leave. 'Hold on', I said, 'I am reaching'. All the people that I asked for the location kept telling me that it was just five minutes away. I ran for good fifteen minutes, somewhat out of breath. People looking at me must have felt that I must have seen my father-in-law running after me with a big rifle. Huffing and puffing, I kept running and spanned almost the whole gamut of the area. Few people must have thought that I must have pick pocketed or something. I was almost there but could not locate the very spot in the concrete maze. I realized how 'geographically challenged' we were at that point in time. We both were still talking on the phone, explaining that we were outside Mc Donald's. I described her about the shops nearby and she did not have a clue. I had no clue what she was talking about, but then we realized that there are more than one Mac Donald's in the vicinity. We were running out of time, and I over ran, leaving behind the Mc Donald where I was supposed to be. Ah! I wondered - was I really loving it!

I again ran for long, towards her and reached in the nick of time. There she was. The running was over but my heart was beating like a jungle drum. We were seeing each other after a long time. She hugged me with one hand across my waist reluctantly. I wanted to take her in my arms and squeeze her gently, but somehow had to resist doing that in a public place - there were people around. It was a brief ten minutes of meeting. She told me she was leaving for Jaipur for two days with her dad via car in the afternoon. We could barely talk but I remember her eyes peering into me. Her dad called up as he had reached and she left. I stole her glance while she was leaving, and her mesmerizing eyes kept telling me that we were secretly bonded to each other and that nothing could come our way. She asked me to please come to meet her.

She was leaving for Jaipur with her dad who had to attend a conference. She asked me if I could make it there as she would be able to spend the entire day with me. How could I have declined that? I had to cover around 260 kilometers by road. It was biting cold in the night. And I was wearing a jeans, a full sleeves burgundy sweat t-shirt with a reversible beige corduroy jacket over it. It wasn't enough to warm, but I was brimming with confidence that nothing could stop me from reaching her. I went back to my place to get my bags and then reached the bus stand. I got the ticket to Jaipur and the bus was to leave in some time. My stomach was rumbling audibly and it growled with ferocious hunger. I had not eaten properly for the entire day. I got a whiff of some delicious curry from a small restaurant nearby. The place was swarming with chattering and chortling people occupying most of the tables. I did not go there with any specific desire to eat or drink anything and I casually looked around to spot something good on the neighboring over-burdened tables. When food was bought, I binged on some pungent and spicy meat and biryani along with coke. Such hearty and savory meal gives a sense of comfort and fulfillment during cold months. I shoved it all through my mouth into my stomach, and at the end of the meal, I was giddily replete. The meal was ok – somewhat spicy. I then walked towards the bus stand.

When I saw the bus, I realized that I would have a ride of my lifetime. I got a seat somewhere in the middle of the bus. It was an aisle seat with a burly man sitting next to the window. The bus started with a deafening roar and shudder. It stuttered and wobbled. I felt like I was sitting on a generator. When it crossed the city limits to hit the highway to Jaipur, the driver managed to crank it up to eighty to ninety kilometers per hour. The driver must have been insane as he was continuously honking. As I had already mentioned, I despised people honking so much but somehow I kept mum. After all, the driver was doing well enough in negotiating every curve with heavy vehicles tooting in the opposite direction, in pitch dark shrouded with dense fog and poor visibility.

The bus squeaked, growled and squealed but it kept moving on those bumpy rides. I cringed and cribbed and held my bags close to me, one on my lap and the other beneath the seat. The spaces between the seats could hardly let my limbs to move and the bitter cold that was getting fierce was wrecking havoc on my bones. My cheeks and nose were cold and teeth chattered. I looked around to see if any window pane was open. Of course not! As no one would have been that stupid. I thought I would freeze till morning. The floor was littered with peanut shells, orange peels and other waste frittered all over. To make matters worse a foul smell was emanating from somewhere that churned my stomach. It smelt like puke. There was a faint smell of that peculiar vomit in the air for a long time. Occasional jerks and constant snoring from the guy seated next to me, abstained me from catching a catnap. We were constantly and mercilessly jabbing ours elbows for the space between. After a while he gave up and I got to rest my elbow. That was my victory, but it was short-lived, because soon to my horror, he began his farting sessions. He had a smirk on his face. What a vengeance? Trust me! It would have done wonders for someone suffering from sinus. I wished someone to have injected me with some vaccine or something that would have numbed all my senses for next few hours. I thought of protruding my head from the window to get some fresh air but it was damn cold, and then I did not have a window seat as well.

It was a real struggle and I could barely get any sleep. I endured it submissively. These are just a few things that one has to go through, when in love. 'The path to love is not easy'. I realized how stupidly philosophical I got at times.

Dawn cracked with unusual rupture, and the bus braked with a long squeal coming to a grinding halt. It was somewhere around five twenty in the morning on reaching Jaipur. My senses were numbed in stillness by sitting upright all night. My entire body had given up, and my almost swollen ass was aching. I was damn sleepy, and with queasy feeling, bleary eyes and thick face, managed to somehow disembark straight in t he hazy mist, to head for a cup of tea. Milky and flavored with cardamom, it was refreshingly tasty, earthy and rich. The weather was chilly and I was breathing out white frost. While having tea I asked the tea vendor about rooms and lodges available for cheap. He called upon a clumsy looking frail guy, dressed scruffily, who took me to a guest-house. While covering the walking distance, I clarified with him that I would see the place first and would check in only if I liked it.

It was a haphazardly built, dingy looking lodge with mid-size nondescript rooms. The old rambling must have been bat-infested. The room shown to me was on the first floor. The door creaked from the hinges. The room had a double bed covered with clean white sheet. There were two chairs and a dust laden small table, along with a derelict wooden dressing table with cracked mirror and other such trappings. The ceiling and flaking plaster walls had cracks with chipped paints. The room had vinyl carpet flooring, stained and battered. The window on the opposite side was open to the narrow cobbled street below, which I guessed would be a busy in the day time. There was also a 21 inch television in the corner. I checked the bathroom and toilet which boasted of western commode and hot water geyser. It was manageable. What made me happy was the tissue roll that I saw. At least, my hand won't face any humiliation, though I never felt using fingers was abhorrent. There's nothing gross about it. It's just a way of life.

And as it was just a matter of spending few more hours. Also, I had no energy to check any other place. I decided to stay. The clumsy guy was grinning. He must have received some meager commission from the reception. After scuttling my bags down, the first thing that I did was to send a message to Nivya about my whereabouts. I called room service and asked for a fresh pillow and blanket. The boy got them in a flash. I bolted the creaking door sagging on the hinges from inside. I wanted to desperately empty my bowel, as my stomach had a squirmy feeling after having chai. I tossed my shoes around, wore my slippers, and was quick to have layers of tissue papers over the plastic rim before sitting on the porcelain commode in the toilet with pants down around my ankles. I shat with shattering speed. My ass was on fire, and to be precise it was on the insides. It had simply reached supercritical temperature. I was glad no one got to witness that shit storm. Nothing but repercussion it was, of all the greasy, spicy, rich buttery meal, that I had kind of relished and perhaps over ate at that roadside *dhaba* before boarding the bus. I shat like a bull and was worried I would clog the drainage pipe. I ejaculated some protruding pieces of thick chunks and some were long enough to make me believe that I was a snake charmer. All done and the gurgling in my stomach and tiny splashing sounds of those chunks hitting the water stopped, I felt great relief and blessed. It was deliverance.

After answering to an unusual nature's call and getting fresh, I sneaked in the blanket lying diagonally on the sagging bed. I felt better. It was a new place and I was alone in the room. Six o'clock in the morning. I was thinking about Nivya. It had been more than a year since we had last met. Of course, I had seen her a day before in Delhi, but that wasn't enough. I couldn't wait to see her again. But I was tired and had to sleep. The cold climate was so conducive that in no time I slumbered to a sweet sleep thinking about Nivya.

Waking up from lull at around nine and rubbing sleep from my eyes, I indolently called room service for a hot cup of tea. I lunged out of bed to unzip my bag to get tooth brush, paste, shaving kit, and shower gel. Dragging myself to the bathroom, I splashed water on my face and rinsed before brushing my teeth standing before the basin. It was time to mow the lawn. I usually prefer keeping light stubble but it had overgrown a bit. Squeezing the gel out of the tube on the soft bristles I started working up the foam softening the hair and making the skin supple. I shaved first in the direction of the growth, lathered again and then shaved against the growth. In such cold it was a real pain in the neck. I stepped into the shower pounding hot water against my body. It felt so nice. And just as usual, while I was enjoying the scalding water in leisure, my mobile phone lying on the bed rang. Wrapping the towel by my waist with a loose loop, I frantically came out the bathroom to reach for Nivya's call. She quickly told me about her plans and said that her dad would be attending the conference in next one hour. She said she would be free for around three hours and then she would have to go back for lunch and can come again to meet me. She was put up with her dad in Sheraton, one of the luxurious five star hotels in Jaipur. And there I was in a grimy cottage spending time alone, all eager to see her. I got ready in front of the cracked mirror and realized that my skin and lips were dry. I wasn't carrying any moisturizing cream or something. I believed that Nivya would be carrying it with her in her handbag. I locked the door from outside keeping the keys with me and walked out.

I got first glimpse of the pink city as I walked out. It was bright, and climate extremely pleasant, with sun perpetually hidden from view. I took a cycle rickshaw that passed through a maze of cluttered and colorful bazaar, with brisk air frisking my ears. At times swerving narrowly to avoid cows with massive horns meandering and occupying their territory on the dusty road, it seemed like a perfect synthesis of ancient, conventional and contemporary city of antiques burnished with time and history. The sight was both picturesque and imposing. I blamed myself for not bringing the camera along. I saw a horde of camels pulling carts, and I was reverberating in a fascinating city that I knew nothing about, and amidst all that I could feel the solitude of glistening sand dunes somewhere at a distance. And in the wintry weather, I inhaled the chillness in the air which was fresh and different. In my heart, I still felt somewhat guilty that I was not able to do something substantial for Nivya. Though I had made it up to her and she realized how much I love her. I was responsible for hurting her though unintentionally. But then we had surpassed situations which weren't easy for us. I had waited to meet her and talk to her and clarify all the doubts that were tottering inside our hearts. Our relationship was on the verge of despair and breakup, that too, for a frivolous issue. I could have not imagined living my life without her. I looked above in the vastness of sky and thanked God for not letting me live that way. I asked God for Nivya. My thoughts digressed as I felt the bumps on the road. There was paraphernalia of naked wires and transformers close to residential and commercial buildings. I heard some hissing sounds followed by wrecking noises and saw dozens of chattering mischievous monkeys jumping overhead on the shades of trees and electrical wires hanging loose. Some red bottom harmless looking beasts were digging their fangs and continually munching something. I wondered how many of them get electrocuted every year. The rickshaw driver insisted me on visiting a monkey temple as it was one of the most popular sites. In my mind, I mumbled, 'no monkey business!' I had no interest in knowing about anything other than Nivya.

Crossing one of the most opulent cinema theatres in the city I realized that Jaipur must have evolved over the years and metamorphosed into a modern commercial hub. I finally reached 'Pizza Hut' at the main market of Jaipur. Pizzas were being dished out everywhere. With the remainder in my wallet, I needed some cash, and there it was. I took out new crispy notes from the ATM, diagonally opposite to the eating joint. While crossing the street, I saw a florist. I bought separate stems of roses for her, each taking shelter in different pockets on the inside of my jacket.

Nivya was waiting at the table she had occupied in the corner. It was quite early at around 10.20 am and the place was unoccupied. She looked beautiful as ever, in black velvet like shawl draped around her shoulder, a pink top and black trouser. She wore a hint of eye liner and a light gloss of lipstick. We met after such a long time, and it was nice to see her smile in spite of all the emotional turmoil that she had gone through. She was still glowing. She got up from her seat to hug me, conveying me silently that all was ok. It felt like we just started from where we left last time. She did not broach the topic but being the person I am, I bought it out to clear all ambiguities. And she said she knew me too well to understand my feelings for her. Let bygones be bygones and start afresh, is what she said. It bought great respite to all the anxiety that I was carrying in my heart all the while. I handed her a stem of rose. She smiled. Our conversation reeled to lighter topics.

We ordered some pizzas and soft drinks. She asked me about my journey and stay. I realized that it was a realm full of surprises and contradictions, tests and revelations. The lonely journey was not that easy, but somehow I had managed. I wanted to be with her, to find intimacy, to reclaim something I feared was lost. And there I was sitting next to her. I handed her another stem. I knew it might look stupidly romantic, I still did it. She smiled again in wonder. She had warned me to be careful about what I ate outside. Clearing my throat, I managed to change the topic. We ate some veg pizzas. Nivya had always preferred vegetarian food. She had tried meat but never liked it or acquired the taste. It was ok with me, as she had no issues with me eating non vegetarian food. She said that after marriage, she would like to cook variety of food for me, and moreover she would anticipate a positive reaction every time. Wow! I said as we shared our pizzas. Though brief, we shared some wonderful time together. I took another stem and placed it near her plate. That made it three. She smiled and must have been wondering what I was up to. She told me that she will have to leave for an hour or so, to meet her dad, and then come back again. I never wanted her to leave. She said she will try her best to come back as early as possible. We decided the time and place to meet again. I handed her another stem. We walked out to the road where her dad had sent a car to fetch her.

An hour later, I was alone, sitting and waiting for her. In my head I continued to cut and rearrange images of the time we had spent together while having brunch. There was a soft careful knock on the door. It was Nivya who had made it to that nondescript hotel room. We couldn't suppress our fervor to see each other. The ordinary place had become all so special.

We were in a closed room, at peace: together, alone, unhindered and free. The sun trickled through the tree from the window and created a swathe of yellow light. I stared at her for a moment and noticed her hair had turned into a lovely hue. There was a straightforward, clear-eyed perception in her gaze that was drawing me towards her. It increased my heartbeat and shot an adrenaline like substance rushing through my veins. I advanced towards her, with every footstep measured and unhurried. She moved just slightly, slowly, till we got absolutely close to each other. I ruffled her long tresses of hair and held her face in my hands of affection. We kept gazing deeply for a long time in each other's eyes, and we saw our own reflection. I touched her on her arms and she had goose bumps that I caressed with my fingers. I noticed that she was wearing little makeup, just a touch of eye shadow and mascara to accentuate her eyes and lip gloss. It was breathtaking. Her hair ran like silk through my fingers. I delicately pulled her towards me. I could feel her heartbeat as though it were mine. My heart swelled with so much of love I thought it might just burst. I found her lips luscious - that pulled at the corner and formed a smile. I guess butterflies were ragging war in her tummy. She slipped her arms into mine and leaned closer looking at me. The breath she exhaled was the breath that I inhaled. We were inhaling and exhaling each other's breath. I could feel her body tremble, as heat filled every part of her body, searing her skin. I could hear her voice raspy with yearning when I caressed the edge of her quivering lips with my index finger. She closed her eyes. Her breath was coming in short, soft gasps. And with our breath intermingled, I kissed her delicate lips with my somewhat parched lips. Her taste was exquisite, something like figs drenched in honey and fresh ginger. I took my time savoring the taste.

Tenderly unzipping, unbuttoning, unbuckling, sliding, and taking off all that we had. It left us desperate, gasping for more. While we were passionately clinging to each other, I tightened my hold on her and carefully scooped her up. Her heart pounded and she clutched me with all her strength and pulled me closer to her. It was a realm where we shed all our inhibitions, and the next moment we felt our tongues exploring and slithering inside each other's mouth. We were devouring each other all over, as if there was no tomorrow. It was like we were proclaiming our existence. The velvet like and creamy texture of her skin was warm against me. She heaved a heavy sigh when I kissed her earlobe. It was all so mesmerizing and intoxicating. We had nothing to talk as if love was speaking its own language. That afternoon, silence had allowed our hearts to approach each other and get to know each other better. Desire consumed our body and soul and it seemed like a carnival of dreams, with convulsions of ecstasy in our body. She ran her tongue slowly along the ridge of my ear and whispered, "I love you".

We made love for hours, rolling over each other in coitus of passion. I could feel her contours rise and fall with every breath she took and every touch that I made. We held each other in strong grip when we reached the zenith. I felt the most powerful and dominant than I had ever before. It had a very potent force, making me emerge as someone who had conquered all, and then the very next moment I was vulnerable and defenseless. I made her soft and fragrant breast my pillow where I rested my face and her embrace imbued my body with her sweet odor. It was like an incarnation… it was something like I had experienced in my dreams umpteen times. We were wrapped in each other. A part of me that had seen her, a part of me that had recognized her, and a part of me that had waited for her, was complete.

And that is how love is. I read about it somewhere that it can take us to paradise or to hell, but it will always take us somewhere. Nothing before and nothing behind, hence we just have to accept it, because it is what nurtures our subsistence, because if we reject it, we die of hunger.

And here I was on jeopardy of malnutrition. My mouth was getting terribly dry and I spat blood. My lips were parched and I could not speak properly because of a tube running through my mouth. When I tried to speak, the lump in my throat was unbearable. I was unkempt. Several days' growth of beard peppered my face with dark stubble. My swollen mouth, scalp with stitches on skull and wounds dressed for healing made me look like an insane from a mental asylum. I had lost considerable weight and apparently become too weak.

I would reach for fruit juice or warm water every time my mouth ran dry. I could not eat a morsel of food as I could not chew because of my dislodged jaws and wound. Hence it was difficult to even swallow liquid. Dehydration led to bleeding of mucous membrane, and I began aspirating blood from my nose. To lessen the pain, I was administered more morphine. At times, I lost sensation and had food and liquid along with saliva dribbling out of my tingly numb mouth. Observing me in such state had a disconcerting effect on Mom, but she would sit beside me to wipe all of it with a cloth. One silent cataclysm of a tear trickled down from the corner of my pale eye. It perforated the fragile bag of tears that Mom was carrying and she broke down, as it was extremely painful for her. I wished that she was spared from such anguish.

I received sequential neuro-stimulation therapy on my throat muscles, which improved swallowing function. Yet I was swallowing only agony and coughed only pain. I wondered how

Nivya would have felt if she would have seen me in such condition. I was pining for her from inside. I wanted to see her for once. I wondered where she was, so far away from me unaware. It made my pain all the more unbearable. It was a long ... very long wait ...

She said she missed me a lot and kept longing to be in my arms forever. This was after I had reached Mumbai from Jaipur. She shared that it was the most wonderful time she ever had in her life, something like a dream that had come true. She said she couldn't wait for us to tie the knot.

The time had come and I was getting myself ready for our marriage. After discussion with my family, I told her about my plans. Nivya was happy and wanted to be with me as soon as possible. She then asked me to reply in a 'yes' or 'no'. I asked her what was it all about and she insisted me to reply in a 'yes' or 'no' only, as she wanted to make a decision. She messaged me back that it was a very important decision and she would soon let me know about it. How could I say 'no' to her? So I smiled and replied 'yes', in my affable way. I should have known that a 'yes' or a 'no' could change life forever. If I would have known the question, probably I would have changed my answer. But then, till date, I had no inkling what my 'yes' was for.

One day, I was sitting with Karan in a coffee shop, when I got a call from Nivya. I excused myself away to talk to her. She did not speak. She wept. I kept asking. But she only wept. I asked her if everything was ok. Her cry was soft but irrepressible. She said she was scared ... scared to lose me. I would never be able to forget her voice on that day. She said she missed me and loved me a lot. She disconnected while she wept.

Love is an untamed force. When we try to control it, it destroys us. When we try to understand it, it leaves us feeling lost and confused. They say - you cannot cut the wings of someone you love. Let them fly, is what they say. You cannot hold them back. See, I mentioned how stupidly philosophical I could get at times.

One night, the ring on my mobile had startled me. I took the call to hear a long silence followed by her choking voice. She sobbed and was out of breath. I asked her what happened. She took her time and after a while, she said, "I am leaving for the US tomorrow." A heavy silence fell as my heart sank. The wind died and everything around me became motionless. She asked, "Are you there", and I guess I must have replied 'hmmm' in a low voice. She was crying. I felt a sudden sinking sensation in the pit of my stomach. She said it was a sudden decision she had to take, as her parents had left her with two options. And she opted for further studies in the US rather than getting married to someone of her parent's choice. She had started to slur her consonants, and words smudged into each other.

I was aghast and my eyes that were fixed, welled with a whirl of confusion. I was clueless about all that was happening and I could not understand why she did not tell me about it. I could not fathom that fact. Also, it was not a one-off stray incident. I had not been told about many things until it was too late. I felt betrayed. She took such a crucial decision all by herself, while I was busy making plans for resurrecting my life and getting married to her. Such thoughts of separation never crossed my mind. All crashed down, perfectly. I was stupefied by the reason. My budding confidence and faith were nipped by frost of suspicion. There were so many questions messed up in my mind. How could such a thing happen so suddenly? Why didn't she tell me before? Why was she going abroad? Would she ever come back? What went wrong? What must have compelled her to take such a drastic step? Was it all planned, a conspiracy? I was speculating and drawing all possible theories, but they were all baffling. What hope could I muster? What? With foolish assumptions, I tried to console myself.

Pacing up and down, I wanted to speak with her. I tried calling her frantically, but in vain. All my calls went unanswered. Absurdity cumulated and while crouching in the corner of the room, I gazed at the wall, feeling an enigmatic emptiness surround me. The eerie black night was dead. Torrent of tears oozed out of my eyes and refused to stop. I flinched at the thought of living a life without her. All treasured dreams were crashing and I saw all of them being crushed without a blink. I was angry. I got up. I stomped. I punched the wall hard and hurt my knuckles. The skin peeled off. I sat at the edge of the bed and held my bowed head in my hands with blood dripping from my knuckles. She told me she loved me and that nothing could ever come between us. Not even distance. She said she would try her best to stay in contact and keep me posted about her whereabouts. She took such a vital decision for us… as she wanted to buy time for me.

It was like a stinging slap of failure on my face. I felt neglected, as I could not be an imperative part of her pronouncement. May be she did not feel I was good enough to ask her parents for her hand. It was true. I had been a failure. As the darkness swallowed my pride, I was sordidly depressed and despondent. Life was melting with ashes and dust, and everything was slowly falling apart. I could not evoke trust and confidence in her. It was all leading to an end of something, something that we had wished to last forever.

Somewhere just around midnight, just before she boarded her flight, she called up and spoke hastily with me for a couple of minutes. She said she loved me and would be back after a year, just to be with me. She mentioned all she had dreamt about was to have a family with me. It was just a matter of time and no matter what, she would be back one day to be with me forever. She had never known life beyond that, and live that dream. She said she missed me like crazy and would wait for the time when we would be together.

It was just one of the things that I found difficult to accept. For a moment I thought about people who come back from the US. I could not figure out any. With bitterness in my voice, I asked her, what if at any stage I was dying and calling out her name in frenzy. Will she ever come to know about it? I asked will she come back. My questions were rhetoric. They always were and I guess they would always be so.

She said she wasn't thrilled about her trip at all. It was a difficult decision that she had made. She was anxious – because to immerse in an unknown is always daunting. She was going to a place she had never been before, a place of supposed opportunities... opportunities she hadn't had earlier. And then nothing was sure.

Questions filled me. What was happening? What were we doping? Our paths deviated... we were heading for a journey that had no specific destination. She gave an assurance and confirmed she was meant only and only for me. She said she would live every moment in hope to be in my arms one day. Those words were mere words but they emboldened me to not to lose hope. I affirmed I would wait with bated breath for her to come back. In my heart, I knew that times would change and so would the course of meandering journey, and after all, that she would go through, she would find me... waiting for her. She had not even taken off and I was already imagining about the moment she would be back. How would it be to have her in my embrace after such a long time? That moment of proximity would belong to us. And we would live for that moment. It would bring purpose and complacency to her decision and our relationship. There was sublime silence in our hearts.

There she was stepping out in a new world, and here darkness had walled my vision. I was probing in the dark that I could not even be there to see her off. Before she left, I wished I could have embraced her once, or probably had just felt her touch once or had just got a chance to see her, even if that would have been from a distance. But all I could convey to her over the phone were best wishes to move to the land of plenty, the land of opportunity, and the land of happiness, the one and only - United States of America!

Everything was calm and silent. The next morning my red eyes were testimony to a sleepless and disquieting night. When Mom saw me she asked me if I was ok. I told Mom about Nivya. She had not expected anything of this sort to happen. I told her that there was nothing to worry as she would come back. She did not ask me much about her whereabouts, but when I explained to her the entire situation, her stand was cold. She asked me to forget her. It was not that easy.

I knew how important freedom was for Nivya. All the time when she was in India, she was caged back home and every move of her scrutinized by her over protective parents. Nivya had lived all her life under her parent's surveillance. Her parents failed to understand that their conduct was smothering her. Freedom meant a lot to her, as she needed that air. It was more important to her then basic necessities of life. I was waiting to understand what she would orient herself with this new found freedom. She would see the outside world, far away from the protective barrier and shelter of her parents. I wondered if she was struggling to get used to the unaccustomed culture or had already absorbed the ecological inheritance, ethos and cultural commitment of a rich and prosperous nation. I had no clue. Life trundled on. I could not concentrate on anything. My work was getting affected. Even if I meticulously devised and aligned my schedule and work diligently all day, I would find an element of chaos everywhere. Board rooms became Bored rooms. To hell with company's mission statement, vision statement or whatever crap, is what I felt. I could not understand anything of it. I could not even handle simple tasks, and had stopped being part of the discussions in seminars and periodical review meetings monitoring our progress. I became a chronic forgetter of small things like sending an email or fax and other office routines. It all made me completely lackadaisical.

Trying to understand what star-crossed lovers are, I would spend hours alone on the terrace gazing at the stars, searching for her… but she remained far, absolutely far, refusing to answer to any of my questions. The empty sky above had been the only one I could share my pain with – the pain of missing her so much.

And after each long lonely night, the morning would appear again. I just did not like anything. I had lost appetite and sleep. Every now and then, I would feel those pangs of love and abandonment. Thousands of images and thoughts about so many things would run through my mind, but in no particular order, making no sense. Meaningless, just like my life had become.

Several agonizing weeks passed by, and I heard nothing from her. Every moment I was consciously or unconsciously waiting for her to call. I would go to the café thinking that perhaps she would call somehow by some kind of telepathy feeling that I'd been waiting for her call. And it happened. I could hear her voice and tell that she wasn't too happy. She told me she was staying with her mom at some relative's place in New York, and was soon to find a job and join a university for further studies. It wasn't at all as she had thought it to be. Things were difficult. She said she felt very lonely there and missed me a lot. She wanted to come back to me; however it was not possible for at least a year or so. Her mom wanted to make sure that her daughter settled down. She said that everything was very expensive and it would take her some time to settle down. She could not come online to mail or chat, nor did she have enough money to call. I couldn't call either as she was yet to have a mobile phone with her. After a brief talk, she said that the call might disconnect anytime as she was using a calling card. She asked me about everyone at home and conveyed her regards for mom. She asked for forgiveness and told me to not get angry with her for her decision. It did not make me feel better, but what else could I have done. She was doing it for our sake. She was torn between her parents demanding nature and my love. It made her decisions difficult. But she was determined to get everything. A well settled career, marriage and most importantly her parent's consent. We barely spoke and the call got disconnected.

We lost touch again. For days, for weeks, and I kept waiting. Eventually, Nivya started coming online in the evenings that were mornings there. Again messaging and voice chatting lasted for ten to fifteen minutes, and it left us asking for more. She was using her cousin's computer and could manage to come online when he was not around. Her relatives were not helpful enough and she did not like at all to be there. Using her cousin's computer was like a big obligation. She had never expected all this and wanted to move to a separate place soon. At times, it would get frustrating as she kept getting disconnected and even after spending twenty-thirty minutes, we could not be able to chat properly, and often she left without informing. It was all half baked, tasteless and sour, and always left a bad taste in my mouth. Incomplete, I kept waiting, growing wild in despair.

A ghost of her memory would visit me every night, sitting beside me, sleeping with me. I would hug my pillow thinking it to be her and slept. Every day I woke with a dream, or a thought about her. Hoping against hope, I would start my day. Days drifted away, nameless and directionless like my dreams. I kept waiting for her call. Feeling impelled, I sent her countless gushy and blatantly insipid emails and off lines. Some of them were written in angst, some in desperation and some in pain. Many a times, I would draft an email and then after contemplating delete it. But I kept checking for her emails every day, every night. I opened my inbox only to delete unsolicited spam emails. Those spam emails would only aggravate and annoy me more. I was worried if it would block her email from reaching my inbox. But if she willed, she would have found a way. I had multiple email accounts. She had my passwords to check for the same. We even had a common email account. We sent and received emails to each other from that account. She could have contacted me anyway. She had my home phone and mobile number. Whatever interpretation I derived, the whole drama had a sense of subterfuge. She remained nonchalant about my needs, my desires and my dreams. I could not find peace. I would get restless and my thoughts were driving me crazy.

I found lot of differences and discrepancies in the way she had started thinking and talking. People change with time. She changed too. Her absence was strange and inexplicable. She kept evading my curiosity to know things and I could not understand her nonchalant stance, and found her casual avoidance maddening and provocative at the same time. Desperate to evoke response from her I would ask her if she even remembered me, or knew me at all. It crushed me from the inside - my faith and my trust. Communicating to her left me drained, emotionally and mentally. I was feeling bitter. Seething with resentful curiosity, I tried hard not to let my mind think anything bad and drastic. Staying positive wasn't easy.

Over and over again, on the other side of the ocean, we come across stories of people who travel to unknown places to take up unknown jobs. Millions of illegal immigrants end up doing low jobs, and I had heard about New York restaurants having a ravenous appetite for immigrant workers, legal or illegal. Nivya had taken up a job to support her studies and exorbitant fee, to sustain her living in one of the most expensive cities. She started working in the kitchen in one of the restaurants, washing stacks of dishes and utensils, working by the hour, to earn minimum wage, probably under the hostile stare of waiters and cooks working in the kitchen. It was a demeaning job, but she was left with not much of choice but two – inside the kitchen or outside the kitchen.

I was disturbed, annoyed with myself, with her, with everything - to imagine her hands scrubbing, cleaning and washing dirty dishes of unknown people. It was something unimaginable. She would have never done anything of that sort here. Though things might be automated as dishwashers are extensively used, I did not delve further to know what and how exactly was the work, as she would have felt uncomfortable. She was too devastated to reveal it to me. It was depressing. I was terribly moved to hear it. Of course, no job can be a small job. Work is dignity. I respected her for that, and there she was just going through a difficult phase. It was a matter of survival. But I was not sure whether it was a matter of survival or a desperate attempt to chase the great American dream! Whatever it was, it was one of the times when I resented her parents, for letting their daughter go through such atrocities. What happened to them? She definitely did not deserve such outrageous means. I wished I could hold her hands, and take her away from the taboo life she was living and get her back to India.

She kept telling me that her life was finished and that there was nothing left. Each and every single day was very difficult to live. The picture presented made it difficult to discern the details, as the shades were not easily perceived. One day, during lunch time at my office, I went to a nearby restaurant. I went there alone, without informing my colleagues. While I took the corner table, I constantly kept thinking about Nivya. After a while, I got up from my seat and went to the owner sitting at the cashier table. He knew me as I occasionally visited the place for lunch. I asked him if he would allow me for an hour or so. He felt embarrassed and thought I must have forgotten my wallet or something. He asked me to pay later for the food. I told him that I don't want to eat anything. 'Just one hour!' He thought I was trying to play a prank or something. I could not make him understand, but I told him determinedly that I need just an hour. I pleaded!

When I entered the room I realized it was broiling inside. It was a dim and smelly kitchen. I rolled my sleeves up to my elbow and washed my hands. I stacked dirty plates and put away uneaten food. Amidst the clatter of utensils and swish of water running from the tap, I held my tears in the haze of my misty eyes and washed greasy dishes in the hot sweltering kitchen. Nivya, my heart cried. 'I am with you', I garbled, as I kept washing and cleaning all the stains and oil. Waiters and other guys working laboriously in their uniforms kept looking at me with confused looks. I paid no heed. Though I did it in my own pace, it was quite a task; clearing leftover curries, vegetables, and bones from soiled plates into the bin, scrubbing dishes with sponge and some detergent, washing in scalding soap water, rinsing and wiping with a damp cloth. While doing so I realized how much food is wasted and wished something better could be done to lessen such wastage. All of it went through the drain, seeping and traveling through the bowels of the city into the sea. It was damn suffocating and burning hot inside the kitchen with such poor ventilation and I could feel sweat tricking down from my forehead, neck, and armpits and it drenched my steel grey shirt. The stench emanating was obnoxious, but it had no effect on me and I did well. When I was done, I washed my soggy hands with soap and then wiped them dry with my handkerchief. I smiled at all the guys working in the kitchen looking at me. Those poor guys were from faraway places to earn paltry money for which they kept working hard day and night, sleeping and living in the kitchen where you can't even breathe fresh air. I was touched to think about their lives. It was terribly depressing. Though it was an unwelcome chore they did, no job can be a small job. I tapped a young boy's shoulder looking at me with a smile. As I was about to leave the kitchen, I got a call on my mobile from office and I told them that I would reach in some time. I thanked the owner and stepped out with some kind of strange accomplishment. He must have thought I was crazy and was out of mind. I was.

I would keep looking at Nivya's pictures stored on my laptop and spent time reading her old emails, as I had saved them all as a treasure. I lay on my bed and kept looking at the ceiling for a long time. My heart was in constant, turbulent riot. Time was running out, and everything was drifting apart. There was no communication at all, something that is just so important in a relationship. Be it crisis, or triumph, sharing it in words makes you feel understood, appreciated and loved. Though my life had become cloistered, I was trying to keep alive the fervent flame within. A hope flashed in my mind. I decided that I cannot let things slip away. My instincts told me that she was in trouble and I needed to rescue her. I decided to go to New York and find her and get her back home. No one knew about my plans at home. I could not share it with anyone. Roshni had not been talking to me ever since the episode when I had almost roughed up Abhi. I was not sure if Mom would have liked the idea as she had started disapproving of Nivya, plus I would have burnt a lot of money, but I hardly cared for money. It was something I could earn anytime. I knew nothing about New York. I had no contact with Nivya and was not sure how I would find a way to her. But I was determined. When you get emotionally involved, your logic becomes fuzzy. An overpowering feeling of helplessness encompassed - although my mind swayed from it I knew where my heart belonged. I listened to my heart and spoke to Mom about it. Mom was not sure what I was up to, but as always, though hesitantly, she wished me luck for my endeavor.

I called up Mango. He had been living In Florida for a few years. I told him that I may need his help. When I related to him the whole of the curious circumstance he was more than willing to help me. His assurance gave me the much needed encouragement. I gathered all the information required and I had decided that I would tell Papa and Roshni about it only after getting my VISA stamped. As it was the only big hurdle between Nivya and me.

America's well kept secret has been that it rarely produced enough American-born workers with the requisite science and engineering background to support its knowledge economy. On the other hand, India had been witnessing the brain-drain phenomenon. But there was no way that I could have got a sponsorship for H1B visa as I was not a high-tech professional nor qualified enough. Indian culture somewhat lays a strong emphasis on education and a widely held belief that the greatest thing that a son or a daughter can do is to become a doctor or an engineer. I am none... nobody. The idea of a tourist visa was not convincing, so getting a student visa was one option. I had to prove that I had sufficient funds. There was no way that I could have proved the same if I were to think and do things in a straight way. I contacted my friends to get all relevant information, got a personal loan passed from a bank discreetly so that I could fly. Yet there were not enough funds in my account. I downloaded US immigration and visa forms online, got my credentials manipulated to prove that funds would be available from a reliable financial source to cover my costs of living during the entire period of anticipated study. I realized the power of Photoshop software. I was accepted for a full course of study by an educational institution approved by INS, and I was sent a form I-20A-B, Certificate of Eligibility for Nonimmigrant (F-1) Student Status. It took me a little more than a month to prepare myself, get certificates, documents and required money ready. It all seemed to be endless, exhaustive and overwhelming.

I was preparing myself for this country and cultural differences. I had heard a lot about the nuances to life in the US, but it was something one could only learn by living there. I was aware that I would never lose my roots and will always be an Indian at heart and sing songs from my country wherever I go. Being an Indian would always be my identity. I loved my homeland but I had a reason to leave. I was doing it for love and not for finding green pastures. I wanted to get Nivya back. I was not sure what would happen. I was not sure what people I would meet and what kind of friends I would make and if I would be able to put my arm around their shoulders, the way I do here. Americans believe in personal space. I believe in it too and I wanted myself to get rid of all the preconceived notions, so I took it easy. When all the required leg work was almost done, I told Mom about it. The next day I was about to go for my VISA stamping at the US embassy. I was getting my documents ready and was taking some important print outs. That's when I thought of checking my inbox. I saw Nivya's email lying in my inbox for the last couple of minutes, which meant that she was online for a while. I felt nervous excitement in the pit of my stomach. I opened her email…

Ronnie.

I'll be online tomorrow at 7.30 evening – Indian time.

I miss you.

There was an unabated tide of thoughts in my mind. I postponed going to the embassy for a day. I decided to wait till next evening at 7.30, and when she came online and we chatted for around twenty minutes. She kept on saying the same things over and over. She told me that life had been cruel to her and she only wished to die. I kept asking her repeatedly to tell me what went wrong and all she said was that everything was finished. I told her I was coming. She thought I was saying it all in the heat of the moment. She asked me to not come as I won't be able to do anything. I was vehemently denied. I was finding it difficult to understand her and it wasn't convincing me enough. I had to impel her to speak up. After much persuading, she finally spoke. When she said it, it was something that I couldn't believe. It froze my being and I felt a kind of numbness that spread like a living hell into the deepest recess of my heart and mind. It was difficult to believe. She was married to someone...

The next morning I got her e-mail.

Ronnie. I am sorry for the discomfort I caused you. I am sorry for all of it. I apologize for all the bad that I might have done to you unintentionally. But in my heart, I know that I did not do anything to cause you any sort of pain. I understand that you did a lot for me, and I was always caught up in some problem or the other. But I just want you to know that I too, did care for you and I still do. But situations and circumstances have made life more complicated for me. Anyhow, I know my explanation will not help. But I need you to know that I would never regret meeting you. Rather, I feel happy that at least I came across one person in my life who loved me sincerely and who was always there. I may have been selfish in my own ways, but then life has been worsening. I got caught up with so much that I kind of lost myself in it and you know it. If you can, please try to understand. All I did was hurt you, but it was unintentional, and I am sorry for it. I had your new mobile number but as fate would have had it, I lost that too and hence could not call. Life is no more as it was but I just want you to know that I still care for you. Dreams you had were dreams I had. I wanted them to be fulfilled desperately, but life wanted something different. And by the time I realized what happened, it was a different story. I tried to keep you away from my troubles as I never wanted to hurt you with it or bother you, because I knew all of it would not bring you any happiness. But you probably felt that I was having my way out, which wasn't true. I was just trying hard not to be a problem bundle for you, but I guess I still ended that way. I too was genuine in all that I was trying to do, but life got impatient. I know that you love me, but I've known no one till now who could have understood me and my troubles. I thought maybe you too would take me the way you are taking me just now. I waited patiently for you to do something and you had promised and I did believe and I knew you were making serious efforts but in the mean time my life got screwed and I am sorry for hurting you. You did all you could and I know no one in this world would love me the way you do but I just didn't want to hurt you. Ronnie, I really want you to understand that I did not cheat on you, but life just took its own toll. I wanted everything in a different way with you. I was looking forward to it but it just lost control. And all I want to say now is that I care for you and have few words I would love to say now.

I cherish you my love
You are my dream in this world of hate and ego
I want to scream
I want to run to you
hold your hand one last time
you are my dream and my rhythm divine

my love for you
my heart missed a beat
but I lost you in this world's heat
I'll remember you with tears in my eyes
you were my friend my race against time
my candle in the wind

you were my friend my race against time
my candle against wind

now that I am on my own
I realize I may have many people
But I don't have you
I cry for you and wail for you
All in vain
I have lost my chance and my mind
I wish you were there to hold my hand
And tell me that all is fine

To my love I raise a toast
No love can be as pure as yours
Your love I'll treasure and will remember you each time
Just that I lost you in this world's line

Wish you love. Wish you success
And hope you find everyone but not me
To God I ask for forgiveness
For myself I didn't do justice
But for you I pray
you find someone who can help you forget your worst dream

Ronnie. I don't know what I have written but these words have come directly from my heart. And thanks for your promise in your last mail. Thank you. I have few more things to say but I know you'll not be happy to know them so it's ok. I hope life does better to you and me. I will always love you my own way.

You've been my best friend and my soul mate …

When I read her mail, I thought it was a shallow and pathetic attempt. I could not understand anything. Her thoughts were confused, vague and disoriented. Her reasons were emphatically contradicting and I felt terrible. It was difficult to elude from those imaginations. My head throbbed the more I thought about it. I was burning from within. I was broken... devastated.

I hauled up myself arduously and did not reply to her mail. Countless days passed by and I waited to hear her voice as I had asked her to call me. She was hiding something from me. I started doubting her and shadows of suspicion loomed large. I found it difficult to trust her chastity as I started imagining all sorts of sultry scenes. Distorted facts and ideas were brewing hatred in me. But it was nothing but my ceaseless search for truth. It was my anger and my most expensive indulgence. That anger was not letting me settle down even a bit. I knew it would have some devastating effect. So be it. I was ready to let myself get destroyed.

I was dying every moment to live an insignificant life. It was a meaningless existence – as I was dying every single moment. Staying alone with myself and being plunged in the darkness of an empty room, I sat at the edge of my bed with my face immersed in my hands. Tears streamed down from my eyes. What was wrong with my heart? What if she left? Why was I finding it so difficult to move on? What was it that I couldn't take a breath from weep and breathe normally from the pain that kept choking me in my chest? The only thing that grew in our relation with time was the distance between us. She got married to someone. Everything was over. Dreams were doomed and all imaginations failed. She destroyed it stealthily.

In dark shadows of my loneliness I remained untouched and uninterrupted in my agony. In my anger I condemned her because she broke my trust. I was kept in the dark. She had promised and I believed that she would come back to me someday. Our relationship lost its glory and its meaning. I did not talk about it to anyone at home. I got out of my room with keys in my hand. I stepped my foot firmly on the accelerator, revving up the engine, zooming off without a faintest clue of where I was heading. I wanted to drink like silly till death, intoxicating myself for a heroic defeat! I was not able to bear the pain. I got a bottle of old monk from a wine shop and tried to find a suitable place to park the car and drink.

Without waiting I opened it up and gulped down neat noxious rum directly from the bottle, and its pungent and smoldering flavor, burning me from inside had no whatsoever effect on me. I deliberately drank myself to ferocious lucidity with the intent to get sloshed and get destroyed. And to raise the somber mood, it started drizzling persistently, while I drove the car dangerously in dark. After a while, it started pouring and visibility diminished. I applied brakes and the car came to a screeching halt at the side of the road.

The windscreen wiper blades that were moving ferociously stopped. I got out of the car and walked up a bit. A scream welled in my weary body and wanted a chance to escape. I stretched both my hands towards the sky and howled for a long time like a raging lunatic. I screamed and howled for long. It was like a voiceless scream, as nobody could hear it. Nobody was there. Feeling small and lonely, my silhouette was that of a broken heart. It was as if resonances of cruel fate had hit me.

With arms outstretched, I leaned back straight to fall, offering some stupid sacrifice to gravity, letting it do what it does best. In slow motion, my body sliced through the air and I fell flat on my back against the ground, splashing water. I lay on the road awash with rainwater – resembling a man who had lost in life, defeated and dispirited.

The wind was so sad that it would have moved even a mighty heart. I could not help but cry as I had kept them for long in my heart. Tears swept down from the corner of my eye merging with the rain droplets unto the ground. Unexpressed and inarticulate emotions were waiting to explode as my soul disintegrated into flames. Thunder ricocheted along with lightning. The sound was loud as if the floodgates of hell had burst open. It poured and I cried hysterically to vent out pain that was clogged inside. My tears would have in no way bought any respite to my disarrayed soul... still I howled. The screams cut across the sky into the futile darkness. I never knew so much grief was bottled inside me.

Tormenting rain that was piercing compelled my eyelids to shut. I lay in silence trying hard to stop the tumult of thoughts that was reeling in my mind. Distorted patterns of images and sounds layered over my disturbed frame of mind. There was a rush of feelings in my heart and stomach. Tears had become unending rivulets. And those rivulets turned into bitter sea of ravenous desires where I was drowning. I had to come to terms with the unthinkable fact - come to terms with the reality that she belonged to someone else and not me, lying naked on the bed of infidel passion with someone she may not even have been in love with.

The storm was getting fierce and had clear intention to torment me. The wind was getting severe and it escaped through my wet shirt and ransacked my body. It felt like sharp agonizing twinge of pain in my heart as if pierced by slings of arrows. I lay on the road like a dead man in the heap of shattered dreams. I knew I would destroy myself.

Another car screeched and came to a halt on the side of the road. Karan and Nazareth were on their way home in their car, when they recognized my car and stopped. Karan saw me lying on the road, and thought I must have met with an accident or something. He got out of his car and hurried towards me. He realized that I was dreadfully drunk. I recognized him. With hoarse voice due to phlegm and swallowed tears, I asked him what he was doing. Without caring to reply he worryingly questioned me about my state. 'I am enjoying the rain', I said. I couldn't show my pain to anyone. I had to appear normal. I told him I am ok and to just let me be there for some time alone. He wanted to lift me but I denied. Actually I was so sloshed that I could not even get up. He used his strength and made me sit up. I looked at Karan. Such a lovely friend he is. I told him – 'Karan, my love… had you been a girl I would have married you'. I laughed. I was absolutely drunk. He was worried to discover my state and must have questioned my sanity or equilibrium. He went back to his car and told Nazareth to drive their car home and he would follow. Nazareth was petrified, but she knew Karan would take care. He insisted her to leave and she reluctantly drove away.

Karan lifted me with all his strength and got my arm around his broad strong shoulders. We walked till the car which was a few distance away and he made me sit in the passenger seat. I don't know what I was saying, but I guess I was foolishly blabbering. I was pretending I was sober and in control. I kept insisting him to take me home as I was tired and wanted to sleep. Karan was holding the door open as my left foot was dangling outside, as if I had forgotten I had one. Once inside, he shut the door and then took on the wheels. My mobile phone lying on the dashboard started vibrating. Karan picked up to check. It was from home. He disconnected and checked the missed calls. There were more than twenty. Dad and Roshni had been calling me for a long time. They must have been worrying as it was well past midnight. He called back and spoke with Roshni. He told her that everything is ok and

he is taking me to his place. I said 'Shut up!' I am not coming to
your place like this. I may have lost my sense but not so much.

Papa opened the door and saw both of us. Thunderstruck! And
by then alcohol had hammered my head completely. I was still
hanging on burly Karan. I felt my body sag against him like a big
damp loaf. Motionless, I remained leaning on him, and for the time
of that moment and breath, I found it difficult to stand on my feet.
I felt cold in my chest to see Papa. I lost my usual sense and my
speech was slurred and incoherent. I gave a lame excuse to Papa
that all of a sudden it started raining and it caught me unaware. I
was unable to hide that I was drunk. Papa, Mom and Roshni had
never imagined that they would get to see me in such a pathetic
and disoriented state. Papa got really annoyed looking at me. He
was unaware of what I was going through. I wanted to tell Papa
that I was not afraid of him but for some reason could not muster
courage to speak with him about anything. I could not stand still
and my clothes and shoes were wet and muddy. While everyone
was looking at me, I stood awkwardly for a while, debating to
quietly withdraw myself. I felt thoroughly foolish and kept looking
down. After a while I stumbled through a garbled excuse and
dropped on the chair with head suspended on the left and hands
dangling on either side. I closed my eyes and felt I could sleep
there all night without moving.

There was long, heavy silence. Then I heard Papa talking to
Karan about me. I interrupted and thanked Karan and told him
that he was a nice guy, a responsible and caring son and also a
dear friend. I told him I was happy for him and Nazareth, because
in spite of all difficulties they had managed to seek comfort in
each other and never ran out of compassion and grace. "Everyone
is proud of you, Karan", I said. Taking deep breath, I was trying
to control the emotions that were burning inside me. My friend
saw a pseudo-motivated person like me suffering and sulking.
Everyone felt I was strong enough to get over it. But I was
finished inside. Papa was upset with me as I splurged and lost

valuable time and money. I'd been a failure in every aspect and I was making everything so miserable. I wanted that spell to be broken but it was just not leaving me. Roshni came with a towel to wipe and dry my face and hair. I asked her about her exams. I told her to study well and get all the accolades as usual from Papa and Mom, and make them feel proud. She was not happy to see me in such inebriated condition. She had an examination the next day and I had upset things for her as always. She asked me to remove my boots as they had become dirty. I got them off. She took it somewhere and I was murmuring that I may have to buy a new pair of shoes. My reactions and emotions were confused. Mom was sad. She knew my pain and the wordless cries within me. Mom must have been worrying in stillness to see me destroy myself. A nameless but serious concern told her that I was moving towards a disaster. An eerie silence pervaded the room.

Karan left. Roshni helped me to my room. I saw my bed and wanted to collapse there and then. Roshni handed me my t-shirt and track pants. She closed the door and went out so that I could change. With great difficulty I got rid of my wet jeans and shirt, and changed my clothes to something dry and comfortable. I started getting hiccups and felt an urge to vomit. But I did not let it out. I fell on my bed on my back with a bang. Roshni came in to collect the wet clothes to be put in the washing machine for cleaning the next day. She must have felt very bad for all that I was doing with my life. When she came back, my voice grew emotional – the way drunk people sound. I told her that Abhi is a nice guy and I will get her married to him one day. She noticed that I had worn the t-shirt inside-out. I was too sloshed to wear it correctly. She adjusted my head on the pillow, spreading a blanket over me; sat on the floor next to the bed with a despairing and worried look, coaxing me to sleep. It was too late, she said. We can talk about it later. I could still hear the rain and the roar of thunder. Why was it not stopping? I did not want my sister to ever go through a heart break as I knew her conviction to love someone. My hiccups got severe and I felt uneasy. I could not hold it and puked on the bed. It was disgusting. I spoiled the blanket and bed sheet and in the melee I hit the vase at the side table and it fell and crashed on the floor with a bang. Papa and Mom rushed in the room.

I dragged myself to the bathroom, opened the commode cover, hunched over it and puked again. Cursing myself to death for what I did, I held the cold rim of the toilet bowl and puked more. I felt very uneasy. I felt I would die. Papa was getting furious and started yelling at everyone at home, as if they were responsible for all of it. I felt tears sting my eyes. I wanted to die. After the vomiting had subsided, I flushed the commode. With lots of dizziness I somehow pulled myself upright. My head was throbbing. Breathing hard, I splashed water on my face in the basin and rinsed my mouth and then drank some water from the tap.

That night slipped into the morning silently and without warning like a thief in the dead of night. When I woke up and climbed out of bed, I never wanted to face the day. I did not feel like watching my face in the mirror. I trudged along with a reeling head recollecting all that happened and thought that it must have been a nightmare. Then I saw my wounded knuckles, the missing lamp from the table, my t-shirt that I was wearing inside-out. My head throbbed and I felt guilty and shameful.

At the breakfast table, no one reacted or asked me anything, as if nothing had happened, and that made me feel even more regretful. A sensation of eerie and familiar silence gripped me for a moment. I guess I had a wistful expression. When Papa left for work and Roshni for her exam, I sat with Mom and spoke to her. I held her hands in mine and promised her that I would never touch alcohol again. She hugged me and said that she trusts me. She said, "I know you have been sincere and have been doing a lot with all the right intent. It is just that things are not happening the way you want them to. But then that's life. Let me also tell you that you are very dear to us and we all love you a lot. You are my *Raja beta*, and I am proud of you'. I clinched on to her and cried. Her embrace was warm and assuring and I felt embarrassed to be still loved by her. I hated myself for it, thinking about my drunken stupor. I wished I had died.

But Death denied me too, and it was an emphatic denial. There was something inside me that did not let me die. May be I was indebted to something. Unbelievably, I was breathing. I lay in bed for seven days in a persistent vegetative state with tubes surgically inserted in my stomach for nutrition, feeding me vital fluids necessary to keep me alive.

In those seven days I came to consciousness few times only to realize that something drastic had happened to me. Then I slumbered to agonizing sleep in the heat of smoldering dreadful dreams. My body seemed to be weakening by the hour and it was all so depressing like hell. Sadness seeped into my bones settling in its marrow. Cloistered in my grave, flesh eating slimy and filthy maggots and hundreds of worms and larvae were creeping and ravenously feasting on the lesions on my face, eyelids, nose, ears, lips, legs, elbows, shoulders, feeding on the live tissues of my open wounds, getting rotten and emanating foul smell. Squirming, congregating in clumps and moving en masses inexhaustibly. Those nasty creatures kept secreting sticky enzymes, vomiting the same congested blood that they sucked on my rotten face and infected mouth. They filled my mouth with a bitter, acidic and repugnant taste. With my body dissolving I thought soon life would depart from the gate of my skull or some aperture. Strange it may sound, but I saw myself standing next to the bed, looking at my body lying motionless in the bed. It invoked revulsion in me and I loathed such dreams, and struggled to escape the clutches of sleep and detach myself from those nightmares that left me exhausted when I found myself in between doleful slumber and half wakefulness.

When I woke up I felt a dainty hand on my arms. I saw Mom. My guilty conscious heart wanted to tell her that I was not drunk. There was no trace of alcohol found in my blood reports. I had kept my promise. Trying hard to recall about the accident, I woke up in the hospital bed in what seemed to be a long sleep amongst a swarm of concerned and bewildered faces. I lay there, sinking deep and low. Syringes with all kinds of weird medicines were injected in my body, and time to time, I could feel a sensation running through my veins to pelvis. A tube was inserted through the abdomen into the stomach, and through this intravenous line, liquid supplements and medicines were given via feeding tube. The intravenous sites were changed every few days to avoid infection. But my body was not able to handle the IV fluids, and it developed swelling in my arms and legs, and fluid in lungs, which made breathing more difficult. My family went through living hell. Their own lives were disrupted, and they had left everything, just to be besides me and pray for me so that I could get back to normal.

Nivedita was not there. She was in a strange world of unknown people and married to someone. I thought my pain might just subside if I would wish for her well being. But the pain was unbearable and I asked for help. I was given intravenous sedative so that I could fall asleep.

With time, so many things slipped away. I began my struggle to deal with uncertainty that predominantly influenced my thought. Lying in the hospital I felt upset, guilty, and angry at myself to having put my family go through so much. At a time where I should have taken control and been responsible towards my family, I became a burden. I didn't deserve the vindication I received but somewhere deep inside I did realize that I needed to make the most of my chance of assimilating myself back into the society and mending relationships I deeply cherished.

I was over and again being hassled by X-rays, blood and other tests. I lay there stuck to my bed almost finished with pain which was forceful and I breathed with aspirated wheezing. Due to nasal congestion, there was an increasing chance of mouth infection as I was breathing most of the air from mouth. It left my mouth dry and my lungs were absorbing germs directly. It slowed down the passage of oxygen in the blood. Bleeding from nose had stopped and the swelling started to subside. Doctors were waiting for this. Nose surgery was critical. Local anesthesia helped the doctor to place a small incision in the mucous membrane of the septum to prevent any damage to cartilage and by pressing his fingers the doctor manipulated the bone to align the minor deviation. It was painful like hell. I couldn't even scream. I wasn't even sure what all was going on. The doctor said it would take around four weeks or so to heal.

I was also told I was fortunate enough to not have any permanent nerve damage. The doctor told me that had my skull not been so thick, I wouldn't have survived the blow. Well what else could have been expected other than a thick skull for a thick head like me? Surgeons were continuously treating the fractures and lacerations on my face, and my jaw bones were surgically adjusted. The bone fragments had damaged the surrounding tissues and blood vessels, causing severe swelling and blood clots. Multiple contusions were evident all over my body including right arm, elbow, and open fractures in the inner of two bones between the knee and the ankle; something called tibia and fibula, something that I had never heard about before. I had an external fixate on the leg to hold the bone in place and underwent multiple skin grafts to cover large tissue avulsions, and a huge slit on the right leg. All of it needed time to heal. It all took its own sweet time.

I had received five absorbable sutures on the inside of my mouth. Three teeth embedded in the bone were knocked off, leaving the sockets open. One of the X-Ray reports indicated that a small piece of broken tooth was still left behind in one of the sockets; hence it required multiple surgical openings of the gum and cutting of the bone with surgical blades to remove the broken fragments by drilling the bone, eventually suturing the sockets. Of course all of this was done after administering local anesthesia. But the aftermath was terribly painful as my cheeks till the socket of my eyes were swollen. It took around a little more than a week, and the stitches were broken down by my body enzymes and got dissolved in a few days. It had caused severe cysts and inflammation. It made swallowing impossible and I was dependent on only juices and lukewarm spice-less soups. Never in my worst melancholic state had I ever thought that all this would happen to me. What had I done to my life?

Time heals it all, is what I kept hearing, so all I had to do was wait for this particular phase of my life to get over. With the constant commotion of people coming and going, I slowly began to feel the walls of the room caving in on me. I was in complete disarray. My face became pale and puffy while I had become too weak. My tattered thin legs could not even hold the weight of my body, and I was ushered into the hands of hospice nurses and ward boys. I had become drawn and haggard and I bore the appearance of a man who was staggered, crushing out of life and hope.

I had never in my life ever fallen seriously ill. It was the first time that I was under so much of medication and care. I was sick of the hospital. I was sick of the strong smell of spirit & phenol that the staff used day and night to obsessively clean the polished floors. I was sick of listening to monitors beeping in slow rhythm. I was sick of echoing murmurs of nurses. Everything about the hospital made it so pathetic. To my left, a paper thin curtain had been dragged halfway across the room, separating me from something bustling on the other side. There was another worried mother sitting beside her daughter. A critically distressed young girl somewhere around 20 – 23 years lay sedated. She had tried to commit suicide by consuming phenol. Strange but true, someone like me couldn't even stand the smell of it, while she had consumed it. Timely medical intervention had saved her. When I woke up next, I saw that the adjacent bed was vacant. She was discharged. She survived.

Even I had survived. Everyone wanted to know how the accident happened. I pretended to recall the accident – I said I had no clue as I went blank when it all happened. But I knew the mental turmoil that I was going through at the time when it all happened. I knew how exactly it happened.

It was one of the late evenings from work at office. There were strange thoughts reeling in my mind – just one of those days when you are kind of done with the sly and spiteful ways of so many people you meet. I could not take it anymore. It all seemed like a city of nicely dressed, well spoken condescending people. It all lied, it all sank, and it all pretended to be meaningful, while in reality it was not. My life had become chaotic, indigent and directionless. I had no idea where I was heading, and what was I supposed to do. While I was walking alone on a dark forlorn road of nothingness, I passed a black swanky car that was parked on the side way, and saw a guy along with a salacious woman making out in the back seat. That guy must have been a filthy rich person. While the woman was being devoured, she looked worn-out and depleted. As I passed by, I caught a fleeting glimpse of that woman looking at me. I did not like her dishonest eyes. They were unfaithful and at the same time had a tinge of pain and repent. The pain in her was so acute, it took my breath away. There were no tears, just deep raw pain. It made me to break the stare and look away. I had nothing to do with what I saw. These things are a common sight to witness in cities, but for some strange reason I felt ruined. It did not evoke any kind of voyeuristic pleasure in me to see a semi nude woman. I just kept walking with heavy steps and reached my bike and kicked off, rambling on those blues.

While I was riding, random thoughts clamored my mind. It had been two months, since I had got Nivya's news of being married to someone. She had committed to coming back to me as virtuous as she was when she had left. But then I had started doubting everything about her. It was nothing but a lie. She married someone. I wondered about that 'someone' she got married to. How it all happened? I was enthralled by feverish thoughts. All of it was hidden from me. How could she do that?

I became embittered. I was paving my way to stagnation and inner death, starved of nourishment. To hell with divinity and chastity, I would hate her all my life – is what I thought. Execrable ethics be dammed, it was a demise of my moral convictions and emotional stability. I was getting destroyed eccentrically inside, and may be my capacity for emotion had started diminishing. It was a demise of my moral convictions and emotional stability. The word 'love' had become forbidden. I was getting intolerant towards it. Fear dried my mouth and hate strangled me, and nothing could justify malice, as I clenched my teeth in angst. Feelings of resentment, bitterness and aversion were destroying me. I was raging with torment of debilitating emotions and thoughts of embracing death. The air got rife with vague suspicion. For some reason, my mind kept drifting to the scene I witnessed and it drew me inexorably to the sight of the woman fucking with the guy in that swanky car. The menacing look in that woman's inimical eyes made her look so deceitful. Disgustingly suffocating, it was smothering and strangling my soul. Wisps of unpleasant scene clouded my consciousness, I imagined Nivya making out with someone in a car. The very thought was repulsive and it moved me from the core, and vehemently so. I felt a piercing stab, not on my back, but straight in my heart. My vision got blurred as tears stung my eyes, and then…

The bang broke the reverie with a rustle, as I lost control. My motorbike diverged from its path at frightening velocity and it skidded with screeching sparks in hair-raising split seconds. The roar and shriek of metal filled my ears. Screech! Bang! Thud! Like an explosion it shattered the silence of the night. I slid for sometime on my face, arms, hip, elbows and knees. Fragments of glass got shattered across and rattled on the tarmac. It caused a trail of smoke and dust to float in the air for a few seconds and settle down once again. Everything went so quiet, and so still, as if in an instant it was all over.

The oil leaked from the engine, while I was lying in a pool of blood that gushed out relentlessly from my mouth and nose. The road seemingly oozed out blood, streaming through the cracks, as if the road itself was wounded. My body temperature may have shot up, as all I could feel was only the heat. With festering wounds, peeled and burnt skin, I lay face down on one side. As the sight was fading, I could see that the impact had cracked the glass of my Casio wrist watch. It showed 22.01, and while it beeped I breathed in short buffs, the sight faded out.

After a few moments, when the sight faded in, I could feel my lungs gasping for breath and I could taste the metallic flavor of blood in my mouth. It took a while for some analytical part of my brain to realize that I had met with an accident. I tried to drag myself up but just couldn't. Locked in a surreal state and with a lot of struggle, I tried to regain my consciousness, and could somehow manage to turn around and lay on my back, on the unrelenting asphalt crossroad.

Floating in space, I could see constellations in the sky. It was somewhat unusual. I saw the obscurity of sky with a distant half and infertile moon, and then my eyes trailed to a new batch of stars gleaming across the horizon that was forcing me in delirium. It shattered into tiny bits like falling stars, causing sleep-inducing strain. It was a timeless descent in slow motion. I could hear her voice. She was calling my name. With sticky eyelids, my entire body shivering, I wished death upon a falling star. Meteorically the beep started fading. It was 22.08 and time was about to cease. My life was ebbing out of me... slowly I was drifting away... A rush of wind, blurred images, echoing sounds of deranged glee and it was finally the end...

The hero in me had died.

A few of the pages of my life's story remained empty and paradoxically, would remain blank forever.

I don't know till date how I was taken to the hospital. Probably after the accident people must have gathered and an ambulance must have appeared. They must have scooped my almost mangled body, had zoomed off in the dark with siren blaring... I was in hospital for almost a month. The accident took a considerable toll on me. When I regained myself, I was transferred to a different floor to begin some rehab then. I choked water and my saliva appeared pale. I lost appetite. I had lost weight. I joined Events in them. I started recuperating, my long road grew slowly on my matted nerves, and slowly being grew on my chin, and I could not even wiggle my feet gently without pain... But more because of the worst in it, I knew I had to muster enough courage and faith to get going and that it would but a time for me to gain my composure and gather my thoughts and my health which were disintegrated for some time. This was the first step to recovery and then began some of the most emotional stint of my life. My recovery was an uphill battle and I had no strength to even stand on my own I was screwy, yet felt convulsions in my body. My legs quivered, and a wave of hot pain surged through my body. The numbness given reduced the pain to quite an extent that I could function within.... And then the way came when I was back to being...My wife then intended using the commode-chair in a day with the front of room to living room.

Mom, Roshni and Papa took care of me too. It was a baby, so irresponsible that I had been. Felt I did not deserve all of that at all. I have never made me realize what ordeal they went through. It had bought them so much of grief and anxiety. Besides, for of money and time was wasted, it was so much, wasted on my parents. They seem to lost their young son. I felt unfit to see my Papa. Life had never been easy for him and I did not do anything.

The hero in me had died.

A few of the pages of my life's story remained empty and paradoxically would remain blank forever...

I don't know till date how I was taken to the hospital. Probably after the accident people must have gathered and an ambulance must have appeared. They must have scooped my almost mangled body and zoomed off in the dark with sirens blaring. I was in hospital for almost a month. The accident took a considerable toll over me. When I regained myself, I was transferred to a different floor to begin some physiotherapy. I looked weary and my skin appeared pale. I lost appetite. I had lost around 12 kilos. Feverish dreams flickered through my eyes, long nails grew slowly on my parched fingers, and shaggy beard grew on my chin, and I could not even sponge my face gently with soap and warm water because of the wounds. I knew I had to muster enough courage and faith to get going and that it would take time for me to gain my composure and gather my thoughts and my health which were disintegrated for some time. This was the first step to recovery and then began some of the most emotional trials of my life. My recovery was an uphill battle and I had no strength to even stand on my own. I was scrawny and felt convulsions in my body. My legs quivered and a wave of intense pain surged through my body. The morphine given reduced the pain to quite an extent still I found it difficult to limp. And then the day came when I was back to home. My privileges included using the commode once in a day walking from bedroom to living room.

Mom, Roshni and Papa took care of me as if I was a baby. So irresponsible that I had been, I felt I did not deserve all of it at all. They never made me realize what ordeal they went through. It had bought them so much of grief and anxiety. Besides, lot of money and time was wasted. It was so much stressful for my parents. They nearly lost their young son. I felt guilty to see my Papa. Life had never been easy for him and I did not do anything to make it better either. There was something that I look up to when I thought about his life as a young man who was suddenly thrown in quandary, when he lost his father, and as a sole earning member had to provide for so many people dependent on him. Those were destabilizing and insecure times, with no property and no savings. Every day was a challenge that he faced fiercely with utmost determination and he was able to support other members till they were all settled. He did so much for our family and never made us realize about his saga and spared us from the ignominy and tribulations that he had encountered during his young days.

When I saw my maimed face and weak broken body in full length mirror, I was devastated to see what I had done to myself. The days that followed were like solitary confinement. Bed ridden with swollen body, I felt very scrawny, as weakness was creeping in my bones and muscles. I could feel the humid dampness while lying on the bed sleeping at odd hours. The bed supposedly to bring comfort seemed morbid. I felt like ripping of the pillows and bed sheet and screaming. My facial expressions stirred and grimaced in frustration and agony. Being awake at nights and with soggy eyes, the insides of my intestines were creating spasms of inexorable pain. I was too weak to even get up for a glass of water when my throat was parched with dryness. I used to get restless, extremely bored and it was all driving me to almost insanity. Roshni would keep coming to my room at nights to make sure all was ok. If she saw me awake, she would ask me if I needed anything. She would sit next to me on the bed and touch my forehead with her palms to check for temperature. If I felt like talking to her and convey her something, I could not do it easily. At times I would just hold her hand and ask her to sit beside for some time. She would ask me, and I would nod her with my pathetic expressions and verbal nods. I guess she understood when I conveyed my apology through my eyes - as I could not be as thoughtful or as receptive as I should have been. I said, 'sorry'. She placed her hand on my mouth gently and hushed me to not talk. She said it was all ok and that I should not worry about it. She must have felt sad as she knew I was feeling devastated. She was aware that Nivya had left me forever and it had affected me adversely. I had turned prosaic the day she left me. Roshni held my hand with both her hands and I saw tears trickle down on her cheeks. She said she wanted her brother back. With moist eyes, I tried to smile and promised her silently. She kissed my hand.

I would lie on my bed in the loneliness of the dark, fighting the pain, until the sun came up, again to drag myself to my feet. While I was trying to summon my strength, I was also waiting for my wounds to heal. The weeks, dreary and painful, dragged by and turned into months. I was asked not to strain my eyes and to not read, watch television or sit in front of the computer. But I could not hold myself to turn on the computer to check for emails in my inbox. It took a while to start. I connected to the internet and logged on to see hundreds of emails, but not the one I was looking for. I cleared them all. I knew one day, she would email me and I kept waiting. While she maintained silence, it did not come easily to me. I hated that silence. I wanted to write to her but I was weak, confused, agitated, hesitant, angry, hurt, impatient, restless, curious, contemplative, and despondent. All in all, I was not in the correct frame of mind. And that wasn't good, so I thought of being silent and wait for some more time. I checked her old emails and kept reading them all one by one.

I turned off the computer and dragged myself to reach my bed and sprawled across, looking outside the window. I saw a constellation in the sky. It appeared diffused. The sky wasn't bright enough. I wondered what that astral projection was all about. There were so many things that I just could not understand. A sense of chronic melancholy kept growing inside me. So many dreams that I had nurtured got crammed with unnecessary traces of deceit and all the possibilities were seemingly far out of reach.

It was difficult and unbearable to think about my life that would be devoid and deprived. My feelings were reduced to unfulfilled desires. I knew I sounded eccentric and impractical as I believed there was no one beyond her. There was no room for anyone else in my heart, as that would have been wrong. But what wrong did I do? If she loved me so much how could she marry someone else? I was asked to forget her. I was told to let it go. But how could I have just let it go. It caused so much of pain. How could I explain it to someone?

I had heard people say that you have to take the good with the bad, and that everything happens for a reason. But I couldn't understand what good it did in destroying my faith. There was nothing left, but the deep painful yearning to shake off that whole desolate dream, to put an end to such miserable and disgraceful life. The door creaked open. I quickly wiped my tears and closed my eyes and pretended to sleep. Mom had come in the room and stood next to the bed to check if all was ok and if I needed anything. I tried to keep my breath steady with one hand resting on my chest. She must have looked around and then after a minute or so, I sensed her footsteps leave the room and the door closed.

Times were changing. Emptiness had become an integral part of my soul, unwilling to leave the deepest cavity of my heart where it resided. Nostalgia gripped me every now and then and I experienced constant birth and death of myriad thoughts and notions. No matter how hard I tried to not let it happen, her thoughts kept haunting me. There was no forgetting. I was consumed by an innate desire to see her, to meet her once. One day.

It had become difficult to get out of my bed. I did not feel like eating anything. Nothing tasted the same. My voice lost its instinctive mirth. I looked diminished, stripped of something essential. Thickened by boredom, I felt no desire to read anything or to listen to music or watch any movie. All of it had made me somewhat insane and I kept thinking about how it all got lost. The question kept nagging me – what made her do all that? I was depleted within. I was struggling my way out of darkness into the light. Days passed by somehow. I thought it would get ok with time but I just could not get her out of my system. Hence her thoughts that had become eternal pearls of pain were something that I decided to keep in my heart forever. There was no other option but to let time heal everything.

And since nothing stays forever, the long silence too had to break. One day, Nivedita called up. This was almost after a year she had left. My heart thumped with unusual beat and I felt a strange nervousness for the first time in talking to her. I did not know how to react or what to say but somehow I managed to strike some conversation with her. She said she was feeling very lonely. She said she missed me! And I thought she was married to someone and had settled down. But nothing that I thought about was true, I suppose. As I don't even know what the truth ever was, as they were all distorted facts. I thought she would never contact me and that I would never come to know about her at all. I had lost her, completely. There was no single trace of her after she had left. She had no idea about what all I went through. I had no clue about whatever happened with her. There was so much of distance, so much of strangeness. Everything was cluttered under a series of misconceptions.

She had come to know that her grandmother after battling a grave illness had passed away. I remember her telling me how she loved her. The pain probably was not just about death. That happens to all living people. Her grandmother must have outlived her cronies. Inconsolable, she felt an inward tumble of depression and guilt that she could not be there, and then being away made it extremely difficult for her to bear those bouts of loneliness. I knew not how to answer, or how to comfort her. I had no words for consolation.

Though miles away, we were talking over the phone after all that was not supposed to happen, happened. She asked me about everyone at home and if there was an addition in my family. There was a dramatic pause in the conversation as I kept silent.

She said that she always kept looking for things in the times that we had spent together. She thought about it every day, and for most of the times, she kept yearning for me. Incoherent though, she tried to talk about her feelings. Even when I tried listening to her patiently, I could not figure out the reason that compelled her to leave me. I could not even figure out the reason for her to crave for me.

When she asked me about my work, I told her that I was between changing career. And then the 'pseudo-philosophical me' told her that I was in love with my failures as it had the tendency to teach more than success. All, as if, I had found exquisite delight in the solidarity of defeat. 'Everyone fails at some point or the other', she tried consoling, telling me that she never found me to be a failure. She trusted my potential. In spite of all the prominent feelings that she said she had about me, I could not find a single word of hers to have an element of encouragement or promise of future.

She said maybe it was destiny's plan – though we couldn't be together, at least we found each other. I found the statement somewhat annoying. But as she spoke there were some thoughts running parallel at the back of my mind, because all the while I had thought that it was destiny that brought us together. Perceptions differ. When we met, it was destiny. When we separated, it was destiny. I started hating the word - destiny. I felt it was just an easy escapist route to avoid further questions and explanations. It was nothing but an excuse. We could manifest destiny, if we become capable of understanding the crux of life. I knew it was a paradoxical statement, as no one understands life. It tends to get too complicated.

There was a time when I seriously used to feel that life could be turned around the way we wanted to, as even the worst catastrophes could be endured with courage and grace. Right endeavor and trust would have helped us accept and negotiate the ebbs and flows of change in our lives. We would have surpassed every difficult situation and bridged troubled waters. And then who is spared? Despair and defeats are part of everyone's life, but we lost without any attempt, without any fight. We lost it. We lost it all. What a bitter irony of fate... destiny... whatever... I guess I was becoming a kind of incorrigible and pathetic philosopher, as whatever thoughts that clamored my mind made no logical conclusion.

"Ronnie, you've been the one who touched my heart... in a special way. I was so engrossed in you and I couldn't think of anything else. And now, that I don't have you, I am lost. Totally! I keep searching for you, but I never find you. I lost you... I am sorry it happened to us."

The statement followed by some pause. I guess she wanted me to say something.

"It's ok Nivedita. I was never there in your scheme of things actually. And then I had not been able to do anything substantial in life. Moreover, had my love been for real – you would have never left me?"

"Don't say that Ronnie. You have loved with all your heart. You still do. It was always so pure. But then things are different now. And I know that you have been kind to me and I always appreciate that. There is something and some part of me always stuck with you ... Here I am, in the hustle bustle, doing just about everything, but not what I really want to, and I don't even know if I come to India, will I be able to see you again. Would you come to see me?" I had no reply.

Was she coming back? My heart raced. But I did not display my excitement or anxiousness about the matter. She said she loved me and had never known anyone who could love her the way I do. She mentioned she would come to India soon.

The sky reverberated like thousands lions roaring, with each flight making their ascent and descent. With so much of anxiety I kept waiting at the arrival gate. The notion was strange to contemplate, and I was wondering about our reactions. I had waited for so long. So many years had passed by, and in my heart I always believed that we would get to meet at some point in time. My mind was racing to retrieve some almost forgotten shard of recollection from my past. So many people were coming and going, dragging huge bags on the carts. I saw some arriving passengers who instantly forgot their long journey as they laughed and hugged their friends and relatives who were in high spirits to receive them. I was waiting, and kept trudging between security check points and the airport security control room. It was taking a long time.

Waiting at the airport brought memories of past instances that flashed across my mind in a whirl - our first meeting... our first coffee together... our first handshake... our first chat over the phone that lasted for almost two hours... our first movie... our first dinner ... our meeting at Delhi airport... corn cobs... bike rides... our first kiss... our meeting in Jaipur... I could smell her fragrance through my memory and could hear her whisper. That was the last time we saw each other. And then she went far away from me. So many sleepless nights I spent pining for her. So many nights I burst into tears, standing in the corner of the room, to suffer silently, to hide it all while breathing the air of poignant desperation. It was all a phase – a very long and dragging phase. It was over. My heart throbbed faster in my chest when I saw her from a distance, beautiful as ever, though her pale green eyes that glittered once seemed lost in the misery of so called fate. I wondered what I looked like to her, and stood there transfixed. We stood still at a distance in silence for a while. I was so lost without her. My heart could never accept that she had gone so far. Miles away from me, she never called up once to ask about me, assuming that everything was fine, assuming that I'll forget her and move on. I would have died alone in the rain. We kept looking at each other. I was still not sure if it was all true, that she had come back for me. My feet were turning sore. Averting my eyes I turned my back on her. I was holding my tears. She came close to me and held me, resting her forehead on my shoulder and cried. I felt her touch on my arms. Had it not been love, I would have not felt the rush in my blood. I turned and embraced her with such a pang in my heart. She almost buried her face in me, and I felt her tears on my neck. I held her without saying a word letting her cry. We remained still for some time, as if the world had stopped for us. Nivya cried, and went weak on her knees and clung on to me, trembling. I held her on. For a moment I thought we would be on our knees. But together we had enough strength to hold on. She kept crying as tears became heavier. She hushed up for a moment, looking at me. Take me home, her green doleful and meek eyes pleaded. I had waited to hear this, but had never imagined it would happen this way. We had never imagined that life would bring us at such a juncture. There were so many things to say yet we couldn't find the words. We embraced again. I held her closer and she tucked her face beneath my chin and cried on my chest, while my tears fell trickled on her hair. I rubbed my hand gently on her back to soothe her. It felt like our tears would wash away our sorrows. So we cried our heart out. Five long years had passed by. People were looking at us, and it gripped the minds of onlookers. We paid no attention. We had to move on together from there, towards happiness that was waiting for us. After we'd been in each other's arms for long, I propped her face up I wiped her tears. I kissed her eye lashes softly, one by one.

And then I opened my eyes only to see nothing. There was absolutely nothing. Nothing of it happened. My infantile passion made me feel delirious. She never came. It was my imagination. I was alone. Again, she remained the mistress of deception. I walked back into my room where I could clearly see my lifeless body on the bed. I woke up, startled, from that dream. It took me a few long seconds to gather where I was. It was 4.16 a.m. I waited a moment for the cloudiness of my brain to disappear. Then I realized it was nothing but a fragment of my forlorn heart's imagination. Though it was a dream, I had tears in my eyes, as if it was all so real, something strange that I experienced. The room was lifeless in that silence.

After months of battling anguish, my wounds were getting healed, but a few scars remained. I felt incongruous inside. And my thoughts were getting bizarre and conflicting. And it did not let me to think in the right direction. Those feelings were getting influenced by thick contradicting emotions. Some obscure force was struggling inside me. I felt no desire to do anything – there was no real purpose. Days turned into weeks and weeks into fading painful months. My recovery was taking time. There was no way that I could have had abjured or taken a shortcut on this journey that was arduous, tricky and painful.

I mused over my unshaven face covered in shaving foam in the mirror and realized that I was not a young boy anymore, but a weak, dejected, and defeated man. Looking at the razor, I was willing to dissect myself and peel all off its layers, to find the core of all peels in its unknown interior. But I guess the idea of dissecting my already depraved and rotten body was not appealing. Long period of inactivity had made me neurotic and impoverished. Countless cells died in my body only to be replaced by new ones.

There was precipitous drop in physical activity. As I was weak in health and could not even walk properly, I was branded as unfit. Practically, traveling would have been an issue with me. Besides, my face was still swollen with pain and scars were not erased completely. I never spoke about my accident to anyone. I did not feel like talking about it. I was turned down in interviews for senior level jobs. Several months passed. I was turned down again and again. Facing rejections was not easy. My parents asked me to have faith. It was a matter of time.

I walked with limp on the promenade and saw many couples huddled to each other, oblivious to the world, watching the sun set. I kept walking at my own slow pace. I had even stopped going somewhere close to that café where love and pride were born, and the same place where feelings and ideals died. I reached somewhere far away from that place. No matter how much I pretended, that suffering never stopped. Dark clouds had covered the sky, and a faint rumble of distant thunder made my heart heavy. Months of idleness had eaten my vivacity. The sadness that gripped me was deeper than anything that had ever been. It just continued to weaken me. I had been bed ridden, jobless, and lifeless for more than a year, with no substance to future and concrete plans and hopes.

I reached the crossroad, where I had met with an accident and fought 'life' and lost once again. Lost in thought, I waited, listening to my heart, beating tiredly and sadly, and kept waiting for a voice - a voice that I wanted to hear. Time passed by and I did not hear that longing voice. I stood meekly to understand the cracks on the empty road that looked dry and barren. A bleak weariness caught my limbs. With shoulders dropped, I got on my knees and touched the ground that was once soiled in blood. I fell into emptiness. The voice changed and turned into rain and poured down from the sky. I drenched in rain again. This time in conscious state, still the voices were mesmerizing, resounded full of joy and suffering, laughter and cries; everything was entwined and connected, entangled a thousand times. I felt as if those screams were spreading their myriad of fear and were trying to clasp my body. Depression was taking over me and I smelt bereavement everywhere. The rain was subsiding. I stepped out of my shoes and removed my socks, and stood bare foot, and bare soul. I felt the rain would completely wipe out the tears inside me… that it would wash away all the angst, all the grief and all the hatred inside me, so that something wonderful and better could take its place. It rained and I stood there with my arms outstretched and face upwards towards the sky, letting it drench me, from the inside, completely.

My mind kept oscillating between hopes and despair, waiting for a bright day. Silver lining is what they say. Life is mixed. Not all days can be gloomy – some days are to be filled with elements of pleasant surprises. This was one such day. It was just after lunch when I was lying on the couch, watching television, browsing through channels, nothing in particular, when Roshni told me that someone had come to see me. She refused to divulge her name. She was smiling. So many names and faces ran across my mind. She said I'll be surprised to see her. My heart skipped a beat as I thought it could be Nivya.

I looked at the door and it was Sanjana. The last when I saw her was at her marriage. She had literally disappeared after that. I was so happy to see her. We greeted each other in gusto. It was such a pleasant surprise. It had been so long. She had moved to Bangalore with her hubby after marriage. She had put on weight but was glowing with glory. She brought a big bouquet of flowers and a big chocolate cake. It was such a pleasant surprise. While we hugged each other, she was shocked to see me - mouth wide open with all that inquisitiveness and worried expression. I made her sit and asked her to relax. You know how dramatic girls can be, a little less than me though. But she was all concern for me.

She had come to Mumbai for a week and through a common friend came to know about my accident. I asked her about Ravi and their daughter Sneha. She had turned six. Mom asked Sanjana about Ravi and Sneha and that she should have got them along. She said that Ravi had some important work to do and Sneha had gone to a relative's place along with her grandmother. Roshni and Mom had seen her snaps on my computer. She wanted to leave in some time but I insisted her to stay back. After having lunch together, we spoke for hours and hours and didn't even realize that it got late in the evening. We spoke about so many things... about our college days and how much fun we had... and how life changed ever since. She was telling us about her life in Bangalore and about her married life. Then I spoke with Ravi over the phone and invited him to come over for dinner. It was so good of him to come. Karan and Nazareth also joined in. It was fun. We all had a good time together.

Though the waiting had begun I had recovered some semblance of my sanity but besides that a lot needed to be covered. The ordeal was a challenge. Being physically vulnerable because of my inability to travel, I could not join any firm with the same job profile as it required extensive traveling. And again as many times I was wondering what unexplainable power was working towards my being. A friend of mine suggested me to join a call centre. The idea was repulsive. I gave it a thought. Willy-nilly, I agreed. Getting a job was easy, though it was never something that I wanted to do. Had I painted the real picture in my CV, I would have not got the job, and would have been ruled out as 'experienced' and 'over qualified'. A few companies where I had applied did not hire MBAs, hence I had to omit that from my resume.

It was a different kind of experience - new job and new colleagues, and while I had been disappointed, nobody in my entourage seemed to notice any difference. I was just there to do my job. Outsourcing might have contributed a great deal for the Indian economy but the fact remained that we had been still cheap labor for the world working on lower wages. I wasn't sure about the future of outsourcing, but then I wasn't sure about my future as well.

No one could see the silence and the darkness inside me. Suffering perhaps was bringing resilience to the fore. My health, and apparently my appearance started improving gradually. The training and subsequent days at job kept me busy and occupied for weeks that followed. Trying to keep a positive frame of mind, I made new friends. Voice and Accent training was quite a revelation and I learnt so much about right syllables, dialects, intonation and inflection. It then followed the process training. I learnt numerous acronyms and jargons. For a person like me who only knew to press control-alt-delete on the keyboard, and think that I was tech savvy enough actually had a lot to learn. Job taught me. Trials and errors were part of the game. It was quite fascinating to get remote access to a customer's computer somewhere in a different country, and check system configuration, trouble shoot, make changes in registry, uninstall and re-install programs, antivirus software and spy wares, and at times formatting the operating system. The process was quite a learning experience. It occurred to me that staying motivated was pivotal for effectiveness.

My work left me with ample of time for myself. There was certain amount of madness in me that had developed to achieve something. All my physical and emotional energy needed a let out. I had wasted money several times before, only to quit the gym each time after a few days. But this time I was determined. I had to regain my physical strength. I got a personal trainer named Hemant. It was quite a challenge. I was distraught by my situation and my muscles were doomed. The first day I gave up, just after fifteen minutes of exercise. And then on consecutive days I tried intense pushups and pull ups. I couldn't do much. But I would diligently turn up every day. I was told that pushups help a lot if you flex hard your pectoral muscles, shoulders, triceps, biceps and even lats and forearms. I had to work really hard, with every muscle swelling in pain at times. I would sit on the bench perspiring looking at well toned bodies and how gracefully they worked out and wondered if I would ever have a body like that. Crunches were the most difficult. Lethargy, as usual tried its best to prevent me, but I did not give way this time. Hemant assisted me in recovery with his constant motivation and pestering. 'Gain comes only after strenuous efforts', is what he kept telling me. We became good friends. I made it a point to work out in a gym for four to five days a week. Slowly I started weight training, stressing more on strength and endurance and indulging more in callisthenic exercises with deep knee bends building thighs, hamstrings and hips and lung power. Gradually, I also started taking care of my diet - rich with high-protein like soya, chicken, eggs and sprouts. I realized I had an uncanny ability to regain lost weight. Little by little, I regained strength and muscular shape. I appeared better and healthy, as if it was some arcane alchemy. This was all because of the right kind of exercise, rest and food which Mom made. All of this would not have been possible without Hemant's assistance and my family's support. I got addicted to food and fitness, consuming conspicuous amount of liquid and juices, to abstain from getting dehydrated. I had recovered from my accident, though I had a slight limp when I walked. It was a matter of few more days, and I knew I would be running regularly and that would help me increase my stamina considerably. I realized the importance of good health and I quickened my pace and tramped on swiftly.

After a short stint I joined another call center with more learning opportunity and better salary. I had to go through almost a month of training. Getting up to yet another morning with sun blistering flamboyantly, and a brand new day to start with, I was looking forward to a new start all over again. It was the first step towards resurrection. I bought some new books, good collection of music, and tried to keep myself occupied. Let it go is what I kept saying. I spent time with my family. Friends were there and I would catch up with them once in a while on some weekend for dinner or movie.

I would sit near my window and look out at the ground where I used to play volleyball – realizing how quickly I had grown up. I also thought about Roshni, that how she had grown up too. Actually, I had been contemplating about so many things, but then after lot of consideration, I did something that I had been reluctant about for quite some time. I called up Abhi and asked him to meet. He suggested, 'let's meet over a cup of coffee somewhere'. I said, 'shut up!'

We met in a bar. I wanted to know how he gets when he drinks. It was one of the weekdays and too early in the evening, somewhere around six-thirty or seven. Abhi had reached ten minutes early than I did. When I saw this bespectacled boyish looking guy, I was still not sure if Roshni was actually serious about it. But then I had to be a good brother and do the best I could. He got up and shook hands with me before we took our seats. I had quit alcohol by then. I had vowed never to touch it after my stupid drunken stupor at home. To my surprise, Abhi had always abstained from drinking. I was not sure if he was actually telling the truth or trying to create a good impression. In fact I was tempted to laugh whenever he opened his mouth but I strongly resisted. I asked him again and he said that he had tasted beer once with friends during college days and he found the taste disgusting. I was not sure about how this milk consuming kid would take care of my sister. We were in a bar reading the menu card filled with all exotic and exquisite wines. I looked around casually and saw a few men drinking pints and at one corner a skimpily dressed girl sitting alone smoking and drinking. I guess she was having scotch. I wanted to know what Abhi thought about it hence I asked him how he liked her legs. And all I could get as a response was a stupid blush. More than that, he was taken a little off guard as he displayed some kind of awkwardness in answering. I don't know what his impression about me had been at that time. He must have thought about me as one of those lusty guys drooling over every other girl, a kind of guy who goes to a bar to pick up ladies and get raucously drunk or something like that. We looked at each other and placed order for strawberry thick shakes. It was kind of funny, may be embarrassing, when it was served to us, and we found ourselves sipping chilled strawberry flavored milk in a bar. What else could I have expected to have with a cartoon sitting next to me?

He asked me why I chose to meet him in a bar when I did not drink. I told him that I thought he drank. With lot of pride, he said, 'Nah! I told you I have always been a teetotaler'. I think I should have got impressed with that. He said we should have met over coffee or something. I told him to not talk about coffee.

'Why?'

'I hate it', I said. And then why cry over milk that's not even spilt, so we lifted our milk glasses and said 'Cheers!'

May be, I was appearing less haughty by then.

Abhi was kind of conscious and it was very evident with the way he was using all the words that he spoke so carefully. I asked him that he should order something to eat if he was hungry. He checked the menu card and after some deliberation ordered for vegetable cheese sandwich. He said he was a pure vegetarian. That did not impress me either. I wondered how Roshni could like such cabbage eating cartoon. I ordered for chicken burger. I was trying to be those snobbish types.

He knew I had come to meet him for a reason. But he was not clear if I had come to talk to him, understand him, help him and Roshni, or warn him about some dire consequences. I did not speak much. I looked at him for a while trying to understand him. He started talking about Roshni. He said, 'Bobo is very fond of you and she is glad to have a brother like you'. 'What? Who's Bobo', I asked. He said sorry and clarified that he meant to say Roshni. I had clenched my fist to knock him down but I resisted. I hated him from the pit of my heart. I wondered why such cartoon guys keep such names for their loved ones. Most of them keep it for cute quotient, but I found it very idiotic. He added, 'Roshni keeps talking about you a lot'. And I had thought that they had stopped meeting and talking to each other. How foolish of me, to have expected that? He continued that he wanted to marry her. But after my accident, Roshni was too distressed and occupied with a demanding situation.

Then he said with utmost sincerity that he likes Roshni for the person that she is and for the ways she's been emotionally attached to the family. Being sensitive enough she was always very particular to never hurt anyone's emotions. To my surprise again, he knew a lot about our family. He had come to see me in the hospital a few times but every time when he visited, I was unconscious, sedated or asleep. He said he was aware of the difficult time that we were going through and his heart ached to see Roshni crying. He also expressed his helplessness at that time and wished that had he been a part of the family he would have been able to take care of everyone. But then he was an outsider as no one in the family knew about him other than me, and that I too had not accepted him. I watched him closely. He kept his hand over my shoulder and said that he was happy to see me, and how he and his family had prayed for me. It made me smile a bit but I suppressed it. Then he said something that I did not expect. He was aware of Nivya. Now why was my story getting popular? For some reason I was getting a little agitated and I gulped the shake in two quick successions.

I had never imagined that Roshni would have shared all this with him. Being a very private person, I found it difficult to appreciate Abhi while he talked about my personal life. And I did not like it when I saw 'pity for me' in his eyes. Abhi was a stranger to me but not to Roshni. I wondered why he couldn't just keep his mouth shut and stop blabbering. I thanked my fortune for that day that he was a teetotaler. I knew I had to cut him off before he spoke anything further. I cleared my throat and said, 'It's all ok now, I am fine' and that 'Nivya is past and forgotten.'

He knew that Roshni would not have gone against family's wishes and had my family not accepted him, their relationship would have come to an end. His words garbled with the bread in his mouth when he said it would be very difficult for him to live his life without her. He left the sandwich half eaten. I was observing him while he was trying to conceal his emotions looking everywhere but at me. There was an awkward silence for a while. Then I asked him about his family and his future plans.

Abhi lived in a joint family. His father along with his younger brother had been in the business of fire alarm and security systems. Being the youngest in his family, he had his elder sister and brother already married. Abhi was pursing charter accountancy and had plans to do MBA in finance. He wanted to settle abroad, as he had no intentions to join the family business. The information was brief but it sufficed to know the background. I told him I would do whatever best I could, and asked him to eat the remaining sandwich. He ate diligently.

The waiter took a long time to get the bill. As soon as the bill arrived he took the wallet out and was quick to grab the bill pressed in between the leather cover. I asked him to return the bill with a not so gentle stare. He obliged and I paid. I realized that Abhi was not all that bad and immature as I had thought him to be. Though I was speculative, I thought that the kid needed a fair chance.

The same night I spoke with Roshni. It was late night and Mom and Papa were already asleep. We were sitting in the hall on the sofa. Abhi had already called her and told her about our meeting. I asked Roshni, 'Do you want to marry Abhi?' She kept silent. How could I ask such a dumb and rhetoric question? But then I inquired how much she knew about Abhi's family. She had been to his place and had met everyone. Thoughtfully, she gave me some insights about his family. There was some family feud brewing between Abhi's father and his elder brother. It had left Abhi disturbed and he wanted to detach himself from the family. Roshni felt that their marriage would make things more complicated and hence it would be better if they bought a separate house of their own. They had considered many things vital for their marriage and had planned accordingly. I liked it when I saw couples planning their future and working towards it. Roshni and Abhi had time in their hands as they were young. I told Roshni that if Abhi was serious about her then they should get engaged, and can marry later. I ensured her that I would speak to Mom and Papa about it. She expressed her concern for their reaction. I assured her that everything would be alright.

THE **CROSS**ROAD

Roshni found Abhi's smile the cutest in the world. I wondered what was wrong with her. I found his smile to be the most idiotic that I had ever seen. My family also agreed to Roshni's idea. And I wondered, what was wrong with all of them. I never liked people for insincerely flattering, that too for no apparent reason. He was looking stupid in that shiny striped grey suit with that awful pink color tie. He asked me if it was ok. I thought of walking up to him to tighten his tie stiff enough and strangulate him. He was actually not looking bad. It was just that I could get contemptibly selfish at times and could not radiate happiness and pass on a bit of appreciation. However, my little sister was looking gorgeous in her glittering attire. Everyone's eyes were on her.

She had worn a pink color pure crepe lehnga choli resplendent with sequins, beads and stone work with matching duppatta and dazzling ornaments. I saw her delicately walking down the steps of the engagement hall with my parents. I realized that my little sister had grown, and was soon to enter into a new realm of her life. It was a strange feeling to imagine her getting married. I was looking at Abhi with, 'If you make her cry, I will make you cry' look. I met so many distant and not so distant relatives and guests. All of them were looking splendidly gorgeous - all decked up for the event. Abhi's parents were very happy. Papa and Mom had got along well with Abhi's family. I had been busy with all the arrangements.

The couple exchanged engagement rings and soon all the well-wishers crammed the stage to congratulate them. The entire family was on the stage. I was called on, and I had a strange semi-grin plastered on my face when photographs were being clicked. Papa was happy and looking nice in his dark blue suit. It wasn't a broad smile that he had but it had depth and gratitude. It was me who had a dry smile, juxtapose, to all genuine and radiating smiles. Sweet as ever, Mom was looking beautiful. She was happy for Roshni, but in her heart was worried about me. Some people reminded me that it was 'my turn' and that I should find a girl for myself as well. A few of them asked if I was seeing someone, and I had no answer to it. I just smiled back at them and with beleaguered confidence avoided the answer. I felt a bit awkward and was murmuring about pretension and perpetuation of all the relatives I had hardly known. Anyhow, everyone seemed to be having a good time. Some of them came to me and pointed towards a few good looking girls, urging me to try my luck. I said all of them were interesting; and so interesting - that I was in no mood to marry just one, but all.

A very elegant looking tall girl in sizzling black and silver saree was very prominent amongst the crowd. Her nose was sharp, big forehead and perfect cheekbones. She was wearing a sleeveless blouse with low back revealing her smooth and fair skin. She was carrying herself with ease and was getting lot of attention, and she was well aware of it. My aunt intervened as a match-maker and almost got me hooked to the same girl in particular. She told me that her parents were on a hunting spree and had expressed interest in me. And if I said a 'yes', then things could be worked out. I wondered if it was really just a matter of saying 'yes'. I mean do such things work out so easily. Anyways, I had noticed her earlier and she was striking, tall, hot and all that. My gut feelings told me that she must have been carrying on with someone else. I told my Chachiji that if I stood adjacent to her, we would look like Siamese twin. I don't know what happened to my sense of humor. She could not understand what I meant to say. I was actually wearing black and even I did not understand what sense it made. I found the situation very tricky and without being rude or something I somehow managed to excuse myself out of it without delving any interest.

Conveniently I isolated myself despite being a part of the merry crowd that was chatting inanely amongst themselves at random. For some reason I was feeling very lonely and wanted to be away from that place and eschew myself from the whole of situation. Just then, Mom came to me and touched my cheek and said that I was looking handsome and that people are noticing me and asking about me. But then she had always been in the habit of saying all this to me. I am not sure if I was actually getting noticed. I don't even know if I wanted to get noticed or not. But it made me feel nice. Mom would always be concerned about me and gave all her attention especially when I needed it the most. Soon she was congratulated by some relatives and they were uttering comments for the traditional silk saree that she was wearing with contrasting colors of green and maroon rich with grand gold intricate designs. She was sparkling in it along with all the gold jewelries. We were all supposed to gather at the banquet as the engagement cake was ready to be cut followed by buffet-style dinner laid out in the adjacent lobby. No alcoholic spirits were served and the food was strictly vegetarian. Food was good and thankfully appreciated by everyone. The flurry of activities had prevented all the gloomy thoughts, but as the engagement ceremony came to an end, they started coming back in full force. All the while, Nivya's thought had been flashing in my mind. I caught a glimpse of me in a big mirror in the banquet to see a contrived smile on my face. It was a pathetic smile. I hated my smile. I found my smile to be the most idiotic.

I saw Roshni demurely sitting next to Abhi. As I walked towards her, some thoughts occurred in my mind. I knew how Roshni would be an ideal wife and a daughter-in-law - a rock like support for her new family. She was bought up with so much of affection, and I wished for her to always get the same kind of love from Abhi and his family. It was a strange feeling as I was happy for her but felt intense sadness to know that she would soon be departing from us. And even though, we would not be living together, the immense mutual bond that we had would stay between us throughout our lives. My love for her had begun even before she had come to this world and I faintly remember the first time I had held her in my lap. I mean so much of time had actually passed and all of that. I knew I would miss her. We hugged each other and I congratulated her. She said, 'thank you Bhaiya'. It was a warm hug full of affection. She showed me the diamond ring in her finger. It was beautiful.

Standing alone on the rocks, near the sea shore, I carefully caressed the diamond encrusted ring that I had bought for Nivya. It was not just a ring, but more than what a poignant heart could fathom. It was a dream.

My thoughts drifted back to those imaginations that we had shared. Nivya had once shared her imagination that on the day of our engagement, she would be looking her best, and how it would get difficult for me to keep my eyes off her. And then while I would be glued on to her she would be solely focused on me. We would somehow manage to get far away from all the attention for some time, to be in each other's arms. I added that may be we would be able to find a quiet corner where we would be able to hold and kiss each other for a long… very long time… may be for hours. She liked the idea and conveyed how beautiful that would be.

Dreary years of her absence did not efface her presence in my heart. I could see her through my mind's eye, when she tousled my hair and kissed me on my lips. But then, I felt that kiss to be tainted, as our relationship had turned vague and shallow, sometimes half empty and apathetic in quality. Just about everything was abhorrent to me. She had chosen the most unfair way of a break up – over an email.

There was nothing left. Delusions of grandeur were all shattered. The only option was to bury those dreams. The sea looked angry; with surging crests of ferocious waves striking the rocks. The diamond on the ring appeared too deep and shallow. Emotionally shattered, I flung the ring far away in the sea. It was as if I was tearing my heart out to hurl it into the sea. It was painful. My heart sank with it in the vast expanse of the ocean and I stood motionless with my eyes closed. I breathed in and out along with the gentle sighing of the waves. Slowly, it got in sync with the sea that was pulling the water in while inhaling and pushing it back to the shore while exhaling. The dream I had was lost in the rough sea, somewhere deep below the layers of realm of time, and I remained in the abyss of my own thoughts.

Marooned, I stood there like a castaway on the shore of imagination, encompassed by a deep sadness. With her photograph in my hand, I fished a liter out of my pocket to set it on fire. Whispering to the winds swirling around me – empty words… betrayal… I held her photograph and saw my emotions being consumed in those flames and then being reduced to ash. It burned a hole in my soul. Coherence was lost in new throbbing reality, and I wished all those things got burnt in my memory. I felt a sudden gush of wind that came rushing that took down everything that came its way. Then I laughed convulsively till I could feel those flames in my eyes.

The past episodes in my life inspired retrospection and introspection. All the mistakes that I had committed were to be taken as an experience. There was enough of wallowing; and I vowed to no more indulge in self-pity and self-condemnation. It never bought any respite. Self-pity was just a matter of conjecture; it was just another disease that needed to be eradicated. It was time to move on. And I had already reminded that to myself so many times earlier as well. Though I did not have any worldly ambitions, it was a new start all over again. It was as if I was under tremendous pressure where I knew that it would either strengthen my character, or simply break my spirit. I had to endure. Somewhere inside, I felt that I was becoming stronger.

I had to get back all the time and money that was wasted. Dad avoided talking about it, but then all the money that was saved to buy a new big house was spent on my surgeries and medicines. He continued with his job and that kept him occupied. His age had mellowed him down and he had become more aware of Roshni and my feelings. Roshni was engaged and her marriage was to take place after a year's time. She had joined a leading finance and mortgage company as a financial analyst. It was a good break and she had started off with a very good compensation package.

I got a call from Abhi one day and he told me that he wanted to talk. We met. He told me he was getting an opportunity to fly to the United States. My blood boiled when someone talked about this country. I knew it was an irrational feeling, may be, but I had a reason for my blasphemy. Anyways I listened to him.

Abhi had always been instinctively fastidious, and I felt most of the times his decisions were impulsive. On a few occasions, I tried telling him not to haste, but my words of wisdom would go down the drain. Like everyone, he too was trying to make an important decision about his life and his future. Being a software engineer, he could dream of only one country. He wanted to fly to the US. I spoke to Roshni the same evening. She knew about Abhi and his H1B visa to leave for the US in a month's time or so. But she had made her mind to not go. She felt our home needed her and she couldn't be away from us for long. Roshni was willing to subjugate her own needs for the sake of our family. I put my arms around her shoulder and told her to trust me. It took me a while to convince her that I was capable enough to take care of Mom and Dad, and that I would be happy to see her settled with Abhi - someone she always desired and loved. I appreciated her willingness and a sense of sacrifice for the family. But then she had a life ahead. She had her reasons but I felt it unnecessary. I never wanted her to go through all that sacrifice and all. Roshni and Abhi were already engaged and it was the right time for them to get married. She reminded me that it was time for me to get married as well. How could I tell her that I did not believe in relationships and commitments when I wanted her to get married? I held her close and promised that the day I find a nice girl, I too would settle down. And then it would be so nice to have Abhi and her come for the marriage.

I sat next to Papa. A father and son spoke. We never had such affable conversation earlier. I felt so fortunate to have someone so understanding as him, and his practical and insightful ways of looking at things. According to religious faith, marriage should not take place till a year's time. But he had his convictions to not let it all happen at the cost of Roshni's future. Roshni was a sensitive girl so we had to be extra sensitive to take care of her feelings. I later called Abhi to fix up a date for our family to meet his parents. We spoke to Abhi's parents and we exchanged our points of view for the engaged couple.

Abhi met me again before the marriage proceedings started, to discuss matters, and how things were supposed to be. With his parents' consent, it was decided to keep it simple. He thanked and hugged me. I asked him gently to take care of Roshni. He hugged me again with a promise and I patted his back gently. I found Abhi to be sincere, and strangely, I had started liking him. I came to realize that he may not have been able to express his deepest emotions, and yet could give so much for a cause or something that he believed in. He could convey a feeling of extreme nonchalance in expression and manner, seeming to take everything in stride with barely a flicker of anxiety. His family too, had been supportive and understanding. It was a low key affair with a few near and dear ones invited for marriage.Roshni and Abhi got married.

It was almost a month later, and Abhi was ready to fly. Roshni and I went to see him off. I wished him good luck and hugged him. It was a different kind of feeling to see Roshni hugging him and cry. The fact that she was married to him had not sunk in till then. They were in love with each other, and it was evident just looking at them.

After Abhi left, Roshni had come over to stay with us for a few days. I got to spend time with her and we went for shopping things that she wanted to take along with her, and then to the US embassy to get her visa stamped and process immigration documents. We had to reach early in the morning. I realized that the queue at the emigration counter was just getting longer and longer. So many people wanted to be there. I was aware that India lacked at many places in creating sufficient opportunities and providing proper system and infrastructure. Frequent power-cuts in many cities, water shortage, and corruption at all levels had been rampant, but as always I held high hopes for the future, however forlorn it may be.

Papa had helped Roshni in packing bags. He also helped her with a check list to make sure everything was organized. I bought dinner of her choice from her choice of restaurant. It was one of those moments that we had shared so many times together – over the dinner table. The food was good, but there was a strange feeling. Roshni was all set and ready to fly. It was time to leave, and the conversations were getting endless. I got all the bags in the boot and backseat of the car, while all got down. Roshni hugged mom and dad. Everyone had tears in their eyes. Then, I went to see her off at the airport. While I was driving, Roshni asked me if I was in contact with Nivya. I said no. She asked me if I wanted her to find out about Nivya. I said no. She asked me if everything was fine. I said yes. She realized I was not interested in pursuing that conversation, so we changed the topic and spoke about other things. When we reached the airport, it was already time to check in. Though I was happy about Roshni, I felt kind of sad as she was about to leave. Why were there so many departures and no arrivals! Hey Ronnie, get real! I mumbled. Roshni had a life of her own and then, for her after marriage, Abhi had to be her first priority. I was not sure when we would get a chance to meet again – may be a couple of years. She told me that she would miss me. She hugged me tight and wept. I did not cry but my eyes were evidently sad. May be I had grown up and had learnt how not to cry. 'Take care,' she said. I nodded a yes. She kissed me on my cheek. I told her to take care of herself and Abhi, and asked her to call up once she reaches safely. I kept looking at her while she walked away with a trolley loaded with bags and suitcases till she was out of sight.

While driving back home I cried. And it made me wonder what had made me so vulnerable. Though I never cried in front of anyone, I still felt it wasn't good. Looking back over my accident, it was like a portent of impending crisis that had come. The past few days were a whirlwind of emotions. Everything at home was in a daze. Lot of money was spent on my recovery and then on Roshni's wedding. All the years, I was dependent on my parents for my survival. The ball game had changed. I wasn't too keen on life as such but I had a reason to live. I had to take care of my parents. There was no way that I could have under any capacity pay back for the years of care and love that they gave us. I promised myself that I would learn to survive, and do whatever best I could for them. I was resentfully conscious of not being able to express myself freely. Mom always loved me unconditionally. Papa on the other hand, had become tender and approachable.

Roshni had left. Papa and I were both working and since my work schedules were odd as most of the times I was doing early morning shifts, we found time together in the evenings. Slowly but gradually we had started talking. I won't say we were friendly enough, but yes, we were catching up on the lost time. A new attachment had started developing and it was finally warming up.

Nivya's thought occupied my mind but I did not let it disturb me. She would find whatever she deserved, and I had decided that I would always wish for her well-being, because to live a spiteful life can be nothing but self-defeating. When her thoughts haunted me, I would try to think about the good times we had together. Slowly, I knew I had to forget her. More than anything else I had to overcome my mental fragility.

My loneliness metamorphosed into solitude and I was learning to live in it. It became an integral part of me. So loyal, that even if I wanted, it never left me. Deep inside, I developed a spring of solitude. This came as a realization and it taught me to love and be at peace with self. It gave me time and chance to know and explore my inner self intimately. It may sound strange but I guess I was falling in love with my solitude. It led me to luxuriously immerse myself in doing things that I always wanted to do. May be it was inspiring, as carrying a smile while dying inside is a sign of strength. Strange emotions took shelter in my heart and they were growing. My inhibitions were gone and I began to follow my heart. I would try to keep myself engrossed. I kept myself busy so that I could not think of her. But it was easy said than done. Deep inside the pain was throbbing and it actually kept growing day by day. I lulled myself into believing that all was well, while I was actually going nowhere. Directionless, days just passed by.

My solitude was momentary. I realized that I had become very intolerant and it took no time to prickle annoyance in me. I became irritable in temperament, particularly when someone talked about love and marriage. In spite of knowing that it wasn't right, I had become a towering pillar of rage and at slightest provocation I would burst into flames. A million thoughts and visions kept speeding through my mind. No matter how long I stood in the cold shower, my blood kept boiling. I could not understand the conflicts of such contradictory thoughts that were raging inside me.

There were times when I asked myself if I wasted my time with her. Why did I even meet her in the first place? How did I get myself so much involved? Whenever I woke up in the morning, the storms that abided deep within kept stirring, and they kept shifting and swirling in dissimilar patterns. All the information that I had about her were so scanty. I knew it was a closed chapter still I tried to find out.

In my relentless quest to find out the truth, I sent an email to Nivedita. She replied. She wrote she had got married to someone on papers for green card. It was all fictitious. The marriage was never consummated. All she wanted was a secure permanent stay in the US; and in the process got entangled in situations one after another that ruined her decision. I was not sure what all happened but she was fighting a legal case to get divorced. She said that the guy was bothering her to not let her set free. I asked her the guy's name who was trying to make her life hell. Someone called Sumeet was married to her on papers and there was no way that she could have proved it to be wrong. Bizarre but true. Some agent that she had come across had made up all the false documents. Sumeet had some devious intentions and Nivya fell in the trap. How weird could it get! I was annoyed to the core. She pleaded with Sumeet to get divorced and to let her go but he denied. He told her that she was too beautiful and good to be left, be it a fake marriage.

All the baseless verbal assault had damaged her confidence and belief; and she decided to not let anyone to be a part of her suffering. She felt she had hurt me enough and was responsible for all the mess that happened in our lives. I tried hard to make her understand that living alone was not easy. There was no way to salvage a guilty mind and her guilt had no resolution. That remorse feeling would not be easy to let go; but it would only come back to taint memories. I asked her to come back as I had a gut feeling that she had been in trouble for a long time. But her bouts of self-recrimination continued. She denied. All my persuasion went in vain and she did not comply with my heartfelt wishes. She had taken umbrage at all the grossly unfair accusations. So much so that she said had stopped trusting anyone or herself to be in any kind of a relation.

Trying to convince me, she said she was mercilessly caught in the whirlpool of life's uncertainties. She wanted to deal with it on her own. She felt no one would want to get married to a divorced woman as it is stigmatized. May be she had doubted if I would accept her after whatever happened. In her suffering, she undermined my abilities. She decided to never come back and wanted to have the last word and that was for me to forget her and move on in life. I was weary and there was no repose to be found. She said that she had moved far away, and had reached a point of no return, though she repented for her decision. She had no idea where life would take her but she was firm on not coming back.

I wanted to help her and do everything that I could have done, but she emphatically said that I should stay away from it, as Sumeet was a rich, powerful and influential person and I could do nothing to him. That was another stab. How more could I get destroyed from inside when I was bluntly made to realize what I wasn't capable of. It was yet another blow to my left over ego. I felt utterly useless and wretched. It added to my anger and agony, but I swallowed silently, once again!

All the thoughts and questions that swirled in my head went unanswered, as it always did. Once again, I could not sleep that night and her words echoed in my ears again and again. I sat near my window, trying to rationalize the turn of events and wondered if life was all about to throw me another challenge. I went for a long walk. I needed to get those cobwebs out of my head. Realizing that I was straying on the path of agony, I resolved to not insist further in Nivedita's life. It was all over.

I came back home. Opening the door, I saw my perfectly messed up room, and realized that it looked much better than my messed up heart. I picked up all my stuff cluttered all over my room and placed them neatly, dusting off old books and CD's. I changed some of the settings, and pulled my bed near the window. And while I was tidying up, trying to reorganize my life, I looked up at this big beautiful poster of an electric guitar that I had on the wall of my room. It had a quote: Love is like guitar. The music may stop now and then, but the strings remain forever.

Music had been my passion ... something that I had lost, long ago. I had nearly forgotten its existence. It had been lying in the corner of my room for so many years, neglected and laden with dust. With its bridge broken and dangling by its string, it had always been an overwhelming sight. I touched its smooth wood and ran my fingers gently on the unvarnished strings. Papa had not liked the idea of me squandering away my time with the guitar, as it had affected my academic pursue while I was in college. He would have not broken my guitar in rage, had I not flunked. But that had happened years ago. It was a different time zone then. I was no more a college going kid. I could no longer ignore it. I had to acknowledge that I was meant for something other than what I had been doing.

There was a burning desire to prove myself. It was time for me to salvage my lost pride. The two choices that I had were – to abandon it or to commit myself to it. I decided to follow my heart, I chose commitment. I held my guitar, plucking each of the six strings running from the tuning pegs, over the nut. It was a strange feeling.

The next day I gave it for repair in a music store and also started inquiring for a new acoustic guitar. I found myself sitting in front of my laptop for hours, listening to music and understanding its concoctions and grandiose ideas. It proved very therapeutic for me and I began composing music extempore. After carefully browsing through a few instruments, I bought a new guitar. When I came home, I showed it to dad. He smiled. It was just what I needed. He said that it was a very nice piece of instrument and that I should take proper care of it. That was good enough encouragement for me.

I took it to my room and settled down in my chair by the window. Strumming once, I adjusted the tension on two strings, and strummed again. Initially, there was some kind of awkwardness as we were trying to get accustomed to each other. I tuned the six strings to its perfect notes – E A D G B and E

I found my escape, playing it relentlessly, mastering variety of styles that eventually became a unique sound. Recounting past incidences, music assumed new rhythms and distinctive cadences. It was for my heart to heal from the pain, and the music that magically got created was something that I aimed to be as soulful as possible. A thought occurred in my mind that maybe I could quit my job and pursue music… something that would be so unconventional, something that would keep me exuberantly alive to lead a self expressed life. It all needed time and perseverance. I had to get rid of my limiting beliefs and then define my true values before beginning to live in tune with them. The process was so intensely personal. I kept myself shut from the outside world to compose music and songs that overflowed from my heart, from my soul, from my core. It became the medium for expressing my imaginations and feelings. It purified and infused peace in my soul. I found my much needed vocation. Days passed by and I made compositions with all intensity, as if there was nothing beyond music. I would record and listen back to the composed songs and music as a critic, and then experiment with variations. It took me several months to gain knowledge about harmony and setting up the tempo along with chord progression, playing around with different rhythm loops and chord patterns. The genre that appealed me the most was Sufi and fusion. But before I could freeze on a particular style, I wanted to explore all the possibilities, thinking that maybe I would create a new genre altogether. I also liked gothic music. I kept exploring, and my musical skills grew.

While I continued with my corporate job, on weekends, along with a few band members, we would have jam sessions, where we had an unstructured approach, making sure that music just flowed, picking up a few verses from some song and giving it a new dimension altogether, on the spur of the moment, deconstructing and constructing it along the way to make it sound like a brilliant new composition. Those jam sessions gave me a platform to experiment in solo as well. Days went by and they remained full, as I was incessantly wrapped up in the serene music and songs of my own life. I was perpetually bubbling with creative impulses with mishmash of various notes that were scattered in my mind. I wrote a few songs, with meticulous music and vocal arrangement, making sure that each song had that magical moment to evoke a sigh, giving each song a prelude, stanza, break, with interlude composed in a completely different mind space, followed by another verse along with chorus…

One day, over the phone, I told Mohit that I would want to launch a music album someday. I had already written and composed seven songs, and had recorded a scratch demo at a friend's studio. But I had no idea about how to launch an album, and I was trying to find a way out. Mohit told me about Meher. He had known her since college days. Though she had made several attempts, she had been solely focused on making her career in music. He felt maybe we could do something together. And then there was no harm in meeting. For some strange reason, he was trying to play a stupid cupid who wanted me to gel well with Meher and pursue a new relationship. I don't know why he thought like that. He told me that it may be a lonely road but if I found someone like minded, the decision might just turn out to be in the best direction. He felt that I should meet her. So he gave me her mobile number and asked me to call her up. Apparently he had spoken with Meher about me as well. God only knows what he must have told her. I had her number for a few days, but with a sense of no strings attached to anything or anyone, I did not call.

Mohit met me after a couple of weeks and asked if I had called Meher. When he got his reply, he put his hand on my shoulder and insisted me to call her. I said 'I will'. The next day, I called her up and heard a voice on the other end. It was a pleasant voice to hear. She told me that she had been waiting for my call. We spoke for a while, and then she asked me about the day and time that would be suitable to meet. I told her that we could meet on any of the weekdays, anytime in the evening, may be around 5.00 or something. She gave me her address and asked if I could come to her place. I said 'yes'.

When I saw her first, she was wearing a peach color long sleeved top with beads of necklaces, which I guess were pearls. She was tall with light caramel curly hair. She was wearing a white head band to keep her hair from getting over her face. All in all, she was quite charming to look at. Her home style too was quite exquisite. I had never seen a house so beautiful before. It had old-style wooden furniture and a distant floral theme throughout. Every furnishing was either antique or designer. It was all done so tastefully, and I admired the embroidery on cushion covers, crimson silk curtains, framed paintings, and embellishment like dried flowers in various colors. The presence and sight of those flowers were absolutely refreshing and I felt like I was walking into the midst of nature. The walls were adorned with non-cramped feel-pastels, off-white, cream and light green colors, and the huge window guaranteed plenty of sunlight and cross ventilation. I noticed the seemingly countless variety of books that lined the wall, shelf after shelf. In short everything that taste suggested and money could buy, was there. She had an enormous collection of music records that occupied almost one entire wall from floor to the ceiling. When I saw a violin kept on a singleton iron wrought round chair, it made me get up and look at it closely. There was some kind of magic that I felt when I ran my fingers through it. Meher had trained herself in classical music and was pursuing singing. She had a very sweet and immaculate voice. She spoke about her work with utmost modesty. I found her to be quite different. She had lent her voice for many advertisement jingles and had worked as a dubbing artiste for animated movies. She also had this unique talent of mimicking sounds of animals, creatures and cartoon characters. So, in a way she was quite entertaining as well. And at the same time she had an underlying sense of maturity and grace.

A maid got two cups of lemon tea along with wafers and cookies to munch, while we were seated comfortably on a divan with big cushions. We spoke about a lot of things in general and yes we realized that we had a lot of things in common. We were initially reluctant, but then soon we started sharing our compositions. Though she wasn't appreciating me profusely, and had maintained a calm decorum, I could sense that she was impressed.

Later, she showed me her room where she did all her creative work. She was also into sketching and painting. Her designs, pencils, markers, stencils, crayons and all kinds of other drawing implements were spread haphazardly all over the place. That was her place to shut herself from the hassles of life and immerse in the world she created to fit her art work. Most of her paintings, she said, did not start with a formed idea. She would listen to music to let it spark the creative flow, and then picking up the brush, would color the layers across the canvas, outlining the shapes, and then bringing life to those images with more and more layers of paint, giving it the required depth and meaning.

She revealed that she wanted to launch her voice; and that she was looking for somebody who could help her with composing music and lyrics. She wanted the album to be somewhat spiritual and offbeat. I wanted to tell her there and then, that I was a wrong choice. What had spirituality got to do with me? I mumbled, but I listened to her intentions. In my mind I was wondering – would an atheist like me be able create magic? But then I didn't even know if I was an atheist… may be I was someone who had lost faith, may be someone who wanted to gain back his lost faith.

But deep inside I also knew that I needed an opportunity, something to lift me from the darkness that had enveloped my life for the last few years. I needed to reignite the lost passion. It was something like I had felt during college days when I believed that I was unstoppable with unlimited possibilities. I did not reply affirmatively but asked for some time to ponder over. She must have realized that I may have my own set of priorities and apprehensions. And I too, wanted to understand what my apprehensions were, and if at all there were any. While I was about to leave she told me, 'Ronnie, you know, there is an NGO, that I am actively involved with, and I don't talk about this to anyone just like that. I don't even know why I am mentioning about this to you, but I think you should come there once. I won't tell you much about it because I would like you to see it for yourself.' I smiled and I said 'ok, I will.' We waved bye to each other. My smile wasn't profound and cheerful, though it was just a neurological reaction to a particular situation, it could have been better. I don't know what was wrong with me. My body language, restrained gesture and voice tonality must have suggested something to her, and I thought that it might have in a way conveyed my aloofness to an extent.

While in college I had done some study on welfares and organizations that were into social services and how it had become a sort of booming business. The mission statements of any charitable and public trust and their nobility of intent would engulf like a tidal wave, but many unscrupulous elements minted money in the name of it. The do-gooders' claims were most often used to mask the ugly reality like money laundering, and using tax-exemption laws to the advantage. Many trusts had been operating as black money laundering outfits. Their modus operandi had been simple. Donations in the form of draft and cheques were sought under Section 80G which legally entitled the donor to tax exemption and the money was subsequently returned in the form of cash after a normal deduction. I always felt it was one of the filthiest ways of making money. Even if I had tried to take any action against them, I would have ended up fighting a pointless legal battle against them for years. Whatever said and done, it was a perfect vehicle to convert unaccounted money reserves into white. But then if a child who's considered to be underprivileged, gets an aid or education, even in a wrong way is not corrupt. It was still noble in a way. What a paradox!

I went with Meher to the school that she felt was so much of her own. And it turned out to be a nice experience. The school was doing a commendable job. It was committed to providing meaningful, relevant, and holistic education to children. Meher explained to me the holistic approach that aimed to call forth from people an intrinsic reverence for life and a passion for learning. The objective was to make learning a fun and enriching experience, and ensure their development of self-esteem. The teachers had a less authoritative approach. They were rather seen as a friend, a mentor or a facilitator, and together with the children they were working towards the common goal. Cooperation had been the norm rather than competition. The school did not believe in the grade system. The emphasis was more on learning and evolving.

Meher strongly felt the need to help the deprived children and to work towards achieving 'Quality Life'. It was an overwhelming experience to understand her genuine endeavor to develop an appropriate level of education, based on the concept of applied knowledge and a holistic approach. One of her regular activities was to organize debate programs on themes such as global warming, culture and values, drug addiction, domestic violence, women empowerment, and other such social and environmental topics. This manifestly facilitated students to think critically about the problems in the society or community, and how to appropriately express oneself and listen with care, compassion and patience while in discussion with their fellow students.

The days that followed were wonderful. Being with those children filled me with an inexhaustible spirit of innocence, peace, joy and love. More than anything else, it was a wonderful experience to spend time with them. A few of them developed special bond with me in no time and I had a dozen of them hollering around, pulling and shoving, clinging on me by my legs, over my shoulder, on my back. It was fun to be like a child – once again.

There was so much to learn from them – being imaginative and endlessly curious. Unfortunately, they were orphans – had no idea about their identity. They were devoid of love and life that kids normally get. They had no idea what their future held for them. Yet, they were so content and enjoyed every bit of what they had in that place where they lived. However small it was, it meant the world to them and it was beautiful. I realized that the opportunity to be joyful is always there. It helped me look at things in a different way, as finding joy is just a matter of choice. I made it a point to visit the school regularly and contribute in whatever way I could, for a cause, that I felt was so meaningful. It proved to be cathartic.

One of the evenings, on a Saturday, some common friends had planned to reach Meher's place for an informal gathering. It was an opportunity to spend a different evening, in the spirit of friendship. Mohit, Karan and Nazareth were also there. We were all sitting on the terrace that had an open garden. Only privileged people have this rarity in a concrete jungle. Open Terrace, that too with a garden – there was fresh, organic cultivation of vegetables - tomatoes, broccoli, capsicum, garlic and variety of chilies. To add to it there was a hammock swing to relax and laze around for hours. The breeze was somewhat humid but as the evening progressed it became pleasant. There was a big mat sprawled in the centre with lots of cushions of different color, shapes and sizes. For appetizers, there were random assortments of snacks, soft drinks, and lots of good music to play. What else could have one asked for – fruits along with tossed salads with different dressings, big bowls of popcorns, salted cashew nuts, pistachios, wafers, along with a few baked and grilled cheese garlic buns. We were all seated in a circular pattern. Munching along, we chatted, giggled, guffawed, while regaling each other with sporadic college time tales, awkward moments, funny moments.

After a while, with everyone's insistence Meher sang a few beautiful songs – her voice, soft and enchanting, floated in the air and filled it with sweetness. She had that poise which conveyed good vocal control. Karan gently elbowed Nazareth and even she volunteered. She took a deep breath to calm her nerves before she sang 'you say it the best, when you say nothing at all...' They were holding each other's hand, and while she sang Karan controlled his blush and looked at her intently and I guess everyone noticed that. We all applauded. The ambience was just right and the mood was elevated. Then, everyone looked at me with anticipation.

I held on to my guitar, close to my chest, and began strumming, playing it clear and crisp, with unadulterated sensuality. I could see everyone grooving and tapping their foot, while I played the strings as if I had an eternal love affair with my guitar, singing my own composition in low baritone, with the music in rhythmic whisper, trying to bring out meaning to each and every word of the song. The song had layers of sublime rendition with melody that was haunting, evocative and timeless. The tune was catchy, something that could keep lingering on the mind for long even after being heard once. It may have transfixed everyone as they were taken over by a sense of euphoria. It would not be an exaggeration if I mentioned that they were spellbound. I closed my eyes to immerse myself into it, taking my sweet time to complete it, mitigating it from the beginning to its completion. It was received with a big round of applause and cheers and it turned out to be an absolute cracker of an evening. It may sound like bragging. But perhaps I needed something like that badly. I was deprived of it for ages and I needed that nourishment. I'd not had anything to brag about for a very long time. But I made a mental note to never make boasting a habit – as self boasting is arrogance. And I had just made a beginning, I had miles to cover. It was just a beginning of a dream where I would sling the electric guitar strap over my shoulder, walk up on the stage up to the microphone and face a huge gathering of cheering audience. The evening was stretched out into a beautiful late night. There was a feeling of contentment yet something was missing. I could not really figure it out.

Few months later...

11th November

The warmth of sun glaring on my face through the glass window woke me up. I rubbed the remnants of sleep from my eyes, got off the bed, rose to my feet and walked quietly towards the window pane and stood there for a while casting a glance at the sky. I looked as far as I could. It was a bright day with sun climbing to its peak hovering over the horizon. Inhaling fresh air, I had learnt to express gratitude in silence. Then I headed to the kitchen and had two glasses of warm water with lemon and honey, followed by a few soaked almonds. And then after getting fresh, I went straight to the gym for a quick work out. It had become a regular routine, and I made sure that I worked out for at least 4-5 days in a week, and spend almost 2 hours every day for workout. I had made it a point to break the routine up judiciously to focus on specific body parts on each day. On this particular day, I worked out exceptionally more than usual, perspiring, and straining every muscle of my body to the limit. Then I came back home.

Papa had also come back after his morning stroll. He was in the hall sitting on the sofa, calmly sipping his morning tea as he read the newspaper. Mom was doing the morning chores. I entered the kitchen. Mom had made single omelet and tea for Papa and served him with two buttered slices of wheat bread. I had muesli with lukewarm milk, a banana, four eggs omelet with two slices of bread. There was inscrutable silence, as we hardly spoke during breakfast. I quickly browsed through the newspaper. Papa got ready to leave for work and after he left, I started getting ready.

I pulled my favorite pair of distressed blue jeans - the one that was torn and worn out in the accident. It occurred to me how some things remain faithful in spite of all catastrophes. This one had been truly immortal. Along with that I wore a smart crisp white cotton shirt with sleeves rolled halfway up the forearm. I was headed towards taking some important decisions.

Upon reaching the office, I walked all the way through the reception area, and then through the corridor to my cubicle. When I reached my workstation, I turned on my computer & typed my resignation letter and then took a printout on a crisp alabaster letterhead. Then I went to my manager and handed over the resignation to him in an envelope. When he read it, he was un-clear for a moment, and asked me if I was serious about it. I was on the verge of getting a considerable increment along with promotion. Though I had hinted him earlier, I explained to him that I needed time for my personal aspirations. And then, in such a big multinational company, I was just one of the employees, and though I had contributed positively, my absence would be felt only for some time, and then I would be forgotten, and someone else would replace my position. Being practical helps; I wasn't indispensible. Nobody could be. The show would go on. I too had to move on. One month notice was essential but being in good terms with my manager allowed me a short notice. I ensured him that I would always be reachable to him for any kind of assistance. He shook hands with me and I thanked him profusely. He had always been very courteous and supportive. He had been the one who gave me critical assignments and tasks to handle independently, and was quite satisfied with my performance. In fact he once mentioned that most of the times I exceeded his expectations. A fleeting expression of pride flickered in my gaze.

He called everyone from the department inside his big glass cabin. Everybody filled in. It was a warm farewell that I received, and I was touched by the affection bestowed upon me by my colleagues and subordinates.

Later, I submitted a copy of my resignation letter in the HR department, signed mandatory documents and gave back my access card. I knew the doors of the company would always be open for me. The security guard opened the door and I left the office – bidding adieu to a high profile job in a leading company to pursue a new dream.

It was about noon. I drove all the way to a place I never thought I would ever visit again. I parked my car some distance away, and preferred to walk. Treacherous rays of the sun were tyrannically ferocious wanting to burn me, but I had the audacity to glare at the sun directly into its eyes without straining. I was wearing aviator sunglasses. That was doing the trick.

Nivedita and I had reached almost at the same time. She had already crossed the road. I was yet to cross. She was standing on the opposite side, constantly looking at me. In stunning glare, while I was crossing the street swerving with fast demonic vehicles, she could not take her eyes off me. Time did not heal the deep cancerous wound in me but it was something I had learned to abnegate with. I crossed the road and strode with élan and gait. I was standing tall and my handsomeness must have been like a punch on someone's face - definitely a punch on someone's face.

She gasped when she said "Hi!" in a half-whisper, unable to conceal an appalling anxiety overwhelming her. I noticed her striking emerald eyes. Her ravishing beauty seemed invincible, though she had a peculiar expression, as if she was peeved, sad, vulnerable, angry over something, longing for my comforting hug, hurt, inquisitive, ready to burn me to ashes, all at the same time. I wondered what she must have been thinking or rather feeling.

Avoiding looking into her eyes, I caught a glimpse of an exquisite pendant on her neck. I knew I couldn't let anything melt, hence my attitude and stance was indifferent. I realized how selfish people become in relationships. They get into a relationship because they feel secure and better. They get out of it because they don't feel secure and better. Simple! Should that be called love? There ought to be another word – may be temptation...! Perhaps an insatiable desire and nothing else... When I lost it, each time I felt I was an epitome of torment. I had been so foolish. How could I fail to notice about so much of real suffering in this crazy world?

But then, my pain had been prominent, because it was only me who had known what I went through and what was left inside me. I had experienced that wrenching pain in my gut. I should have had no regrets as I did the best I could – with utmost sincerity I had tried everything for her, to revive the relationship. Trouble is part of life, and if we don't share it with the person we love we don't give that person a chance to love enough. I could have done a lot, but ... there was no point in even thinking about it. All I knew was that had it not been for my love and for her guilt, she would have not come to meet me.

This is how the story had to end. It had an irrevocable cessation. No matter how much I would have hated to say this, but love was lost in the winds of destiny's plan. I could still not understand destiny's charade or anything about it. All I could realize was that it was over.

For old time's sake, she had asked to come to meet her at the café where we first met. Where was she when I wanted her to listen to me ... to be with me? Where was she when I needed her? My feelings were trampled. I still obliged. Well actually, I did not. I had starved for this very moment, to see her one day, and ask her once. That feeling of betrayal had been tucked in the corner of my heart and its presence had overpowered all the treasured memories that had filled my heart. But I also knew she would not be able to smudge answers to my questions, so no awkward questions as I wasn't interested in any thorny answers. I had come to the cafe after almost five years – five long and poignant years!

Deep within the realms of time, laid a secret, and it was a dark one. She preferred silence. What she must have not realized was that lies are not just spoken with words, but with silence too. Bracing us was the breeze that was gentle, yet prominent. The air was filled with thick secret. The smell that emanated was that of water from marshland, drying out a bit, and it was filled with treachery. A little far away was the sea where I had flung the diamond ring. I could see that tremulous cold blooded contaminated sea where dreams were buried in the sands of harsh times and my fleeting passion got eroded. The sea and its specter had taken on a different character. No matter how hard I tried, my past had kept battering my life like ocean waves, beating and crashing against the shoreline.

I had decided to not let the virtuosity of dark secret that was concealed for so long to creep outside. Even though I had summoned the courage to face it, the lies were stark and it would have only left my heart pervert and sick.

We sat there, not knowing what to say or do. A mildly acrid smell of strong coffee filled the air. We were both looking in different directions, while she kept casting furtive glances in between, unable to hold my eye's attention. Our hearts were hushed and coherent, but the ambience was unnerving.

When the waiter approached, I ordered for a double espresso as I wanted Nivedita to realize that I was not the same person who preferred sweet creamy coffee. I did not pay heed to what she ordered. But I realized she was quick to order without taking time. She placed her hand on the table. I caught a glimpse of her hands - slender fingers with nails perfectly manicured. How I had imagined them to be colored in 'henna' with intricate patterns of love. I wondered how my name got erased from her palm. The ring in her finger was missing. I closed my eyes for a moment when I heard a roar of spurious wave splashing against the rocks on the shore, and then blinked to harsh reality so that I did not drown in the vast nothingness. My eyes were straying elsewhere deliberately. I don't even know what I was looking at... with so much of intensity, like an abstract thinker. My gaze was void as if I was looking beyond the emptiness that filled the air. My presence must have been captivating.

Neither of us spoke. There were no reasons to seek and explain. It was like an unexpected encounter. Silence that was pretentious and wry was broken when coffees were served. Nivedita had ordered for cappuccino. The spoon made tinkling noise on touching the porcelain when stirred with sugar. Espresso was bitter. She was looking at me. I realized how breathtakingly attractive and smart she had been, liberated from my love, drama and emotions. Then something strange occurred to me. I thought - how could someone like strong coffee? I felt as if it was consuming me. I could not imbibe half the espresso, as my bilious stomach could not bear it anymore. It was time for me to leave. I got up and Nivedita was stunned that the meeting was over without anything to say. Stupendous silence was all we shared between us. The silence had left us unspeakable. We were waiting to hear something, something that never came. The silence got louder. She slanted a glance with a lump in her throat, "Where are you going?" There was a complete cessation, and then in an unusual low baritone voice and with no hint of agitation, I told her, 'I need to go somewhere... good bye'. I don't know if she realized it, but for the first time, I said 'good bye' to her.

Her eyes were moist and her contrite and feeble voice said, 'I am sorry Ronnie'. I felt terribly small and hollow to hear that. But it also made me smile. 'You don't need to be sorry. Everything is fine. I am just ok. And yes, I have nothing against you. In fact I am glad to see you. Thank you for coming.' I was looking directly in the embers of her regretful eyes. It was a 'soul penetrating gaze' and must have pierced the core of her being. Putting my right hand forward, I told her I would always be a well wisher for her. She held my hand. I kept my grip gentle though it was a brusque goodbye. I was distraught inside for that moment. My hands that once craved for her touch were numb. After so many years, at the same place, where we met as strangers, we were yet strangers. The purpose of our existence in each other's life would continue to remain a mystery.

I walked away with steely determination to not to look back. She may have cried afterwards. May be… may be not. I walked over countless shattered pieces, and those pieces were of our hearts getting crushed beneath my shoes. I did not look back. It was a breather when I stepped out in the open from that mournfulness of place and time.

Exasperated! I did not let my accumulated pain and feelings to manifest again. For some time I had felt that true love and compassion did not exist. What subsisted in this world was lust, lies, hatred and infidelity in all its form, but in my heart, I knew that true love stays through impediments. People won't stop believing in love. They would never stop wanting to be in love - it's just that every love story has its flavor. Incongruously, some fade away with time.

There may be nothing heroic about me, as it is always easy to formulate an opinion and speak with unchallenged authority about oneself. And that's what I did. Reconstructing facts and illusions, weaving words and feelings, I may have created my own reality, my own perception. And what else did I do? I walked away, without looking back at her. This is how it was supposed to be? May be I suffered because I thought I was giving more than what I was receiving. My love was going unrecognized. The sacred temple of love that I had built within me got stained with blood of betrayal. It was destructed. The sanctity was destroyed. May be it was my karma. May be I deserved all of it. But what had I done to deserve all of it?

Lost in thought, I walked, in the dust and heat of the road, listening to my heart that was beating in despair. The road appeared long and endless. I may have covered some distance when my pace slowed down. It was as if I had walked for miles and had finally reached a turning point.

I found myself in the middle of nowhere - with no sign boards or directions. A painful stagnation descended upon my soul. Unceasing flow of gleaming and intellectual people, burning with lofty ambitions were jostling for space. They were erratically moving in all directions in their quest for life - a mad pace that I may not have been able to get on with. While these people were darting about haphazardly, I stood far behind to decide on the path. Amidst million drifters, I could hear echoes of my own thoughts, and from a distance I saw towering scales of insurmountable high rises. All the buildings around me were getting taller and taller trying their best to make me feel small and insignificant. With dizzying highs and depressing lows, I apprehended that it had been my descent and I may have reached the nadir… every instinct of me must have been crying, as I got fleeting glimpses from people, however it had no affect on me…

I touched my cheeks and my finger tips got wet. The tears were no longer of sorrow or anger; they were not even sign of weakness, but stoic silence that no one could steal. It was just a part of the healing process. I must have reached far. Fixing my teary eyes on the endless road stretched out in a sinister way, I stood akimbo, with chin held up in pride of all the failures I had gone through. I took some time to allow the feeling to convulse me.

My thoughts came from the depths of despair that I reached in love instead of heights of realization. She walked away one day. I did the same. I hammered the last nail on the coffin, to let the so called 'feelings' to rest in peace forever. It did not die a natural death. It died of neglect and betrayal.

I was done with the delusions of the past few years. Though my beliefs had been in jeopardy, I reconciled with the fact that it ended. Nothing to drag along the road now... I was better off alone. Thanks to her - she helped me learn about trust and the importance of being cautious to whom you open your heart. I could have avoided a lot of anguish. As after a few years when I would look back, I would laugh realizing how emotionally stupid I had been. That's how life is.

Reclaiming my inner reality had been tough but an incredible experience. I wondered why this realization took so long to materialize. It was my own slipup – there couldn't be anyone to blame.

I knew there was an uncanny light within me. Though a tiny ray, this innate light in me had been the life in me that had kept rekindling lost hope. Darkness may have endured, but the light kept elucidating, in all circumstances, no matter what, and this small flame of consciousness in me may someday bursts forth to become an infinite source of energy and light.

Leaving behind the reckless pursuit of cutthroat and contemporary life, it was time to find the real purpose of my existence. I had to start believing and thriving on hopes that I could not see earlier, to fight deep inside to live on.

For a long time I stood frozen. A mild wind blew past me when her words drifted on the concurrent stream of my austere thoughts. She told me once, 'often, we take life's crossroad as an end; whereas we should just consider it to be a bend and not the end...'

And here I am, beginning from the end...

On reaching the car I saw my guitar on the backseat. I opened the door and was about to get in when my mobile phone rang. I stood between the open door with my left elbow propped on the roof of the car. It was Meher. She reminded me about the recording for my new music album… All I could comprehend out of my life was that it all happened to give birth to a new musical genius in me.

I looked above at the drifting clouds in the obscure sky, closed my eyes and smiled.

I had never aspired to be a writer. It actually
never occurred to me till I started writing,
but I hope the content is appreciated, as I am still learning.

Thank you from the depth of my heart

V Singh